HER ULT

IDOLIZED SERIES: BOOK 1

SAMANTHA ANN

Edited by PROOF POSITIVE
Cover by KIM CAVRAK
Formating by GARNET CHRISTIE

DEDICATION

To all the No Mac Waffles out there, this is for you. Iykyk.

Also if you're my mom, stop reading right here. I mean it.

HANGUL CHEAT SHEET

Consonants:	Vowels:
ㄱ – g,k	ㅏ – ah
ㄴ – n	ㅐ – ay
ㄷ – d	ㅑ – ya
ㄹ – r,l (say "real" but with an l in the beginning "leal")	ㅒ – yae
ㅁ – m	ㅓ – eo
ㅂ – b	ㅔ – eh
ㅅ – s	ㅕ –yeo
ㅇ – no sound if it starts the word, 'ng' sound if it finishes	ㅗ – o
ㅈ – j	ㅘ –wa
ㅊ – ch	ㅙ –wae
ㅋ – k	ㅚ – oe
ㅌ – t	ㅛ – yo
ㅍ – p	ㅜ – u
ㅎ – h	ㅝ – whoa
ㄲ – gg	ㅞ – we
ㄸ – dd	ㅟ –wi
ㅃ – bb	ㅠ – yu
ㅉ – jj	ㅡ – oo
ㅆ – ss	ㅢ –ui
	ㅣ - ee
	ㅖ -ye

HER ULT OST (ORIGINAL SOUNDTRACK)

Airplane – Stray Kids
Spotlight – VAV
Tell me about your world – msftz
Bite Me – ENHYPEN
Questions – ZELO
Quasi una fantasia – THE BOYZ
Last – Dvwn
Lighthouse – Ha Hyun Sang
Tattoo – Loreen
I Just Can't Stop Loving You – ABLE

PROLOGUE

As the plane's landing gear touched the ground, the spoilers lifted on the wings to create a loud roar as they slowed the aircraft. Ji-Hun peered through the small window to see palm trees lining the runways and highways nearby. Fifteen hours from Seoul to Los Angeles to kick off CLAR1T's first US tour.

This is it, he thought, as he turned to look at his five groupmates, who all had similar excited smiles on their faces. Well, except for Woo Shin. It took a lot for him to even fake a smile lately. Ji-Hun wondered if it was due to the stress of their company asking for him to give them CLAR1T's next big hit. Ji-Hun wasn't jealous of Woo Shin's secret producer alter ego. He had enough to worry about when it came to the group's choreography.

"LA, here we come." Jaehyeong, one of the group's rappers, grabbed at Ji-Hun's wrist and began shaking it excitedly. His personality's duality on stage and off always blew Ji-Hun's mind. One of the youngest of the group had such a rough and tough exterior when performing, but when the stage lights were off, he became like a soft, gentle teddy bear.

"I need a shower," Ji-Hun grumbled, feeling his achy body needed the warmth of steaming hot water to let his muscles relax.

"We have about five hours until the award show tonight." Eunho, their leader, the man who kept them in line but also helped them bend the rules, said as he pulled out his phone to see the time. "We also need to announce we're going to the show. Who wants to tweet?"

"할 거야." Seongjun raised one hand while pulling out his own phone with the other. His fingers flew across the screen, fast as lightning. It's why he was their personal photographer and social media poster. "Posted."

"How does it feel to be back in the states after so many years, Min Hwa?" Ji-hun asked the 막내 as they all stood to grab their bags and deboard the plane.

"이상해…" He trailed off, making it clear he didn't want to talk further about it. He had mentioned how he left on not the best of terms with his family, and he worried that they would try to pull something while he was in the country. They all made a joke that Min Hwa was in the mafia and they would bring him back to the "family business."

"We will protect you." Jaehyeong wrapped his arm around Min's neck, donning Jaehyeong's brightest, most cheerful smile.

"I don't get paid enough to save your ass," Woo Shin grumbled and was the first to get off the plane.

"None of us do." Eunho chuckled as he followed Woo Shin, and Ji-Hun caught their leader give Woo Shin a small nudge, causing Woo Shin to look over at him. No words were said, just a nod from each of them, and Ji-Hun saw some of the tension release from Woo Shin's shoulders. Eunho, forever the dependable, comforting, reliable leader. CLARvoyants called him the dad of the group for a reason.

"What are you hoping to get out of this tour, 형?" Seongjun asked. They all had exited the plane and made their way to customs and baggage claim. The airport felt cramped compared to Incheon. He didn't know why he expected grandeur, but it dimmed his excitement for the trip a tick.

"Perform for more CLARvoyants." Ji-Hun smiled.

"I'm not an interviewer, Ji-Hun-아." Seongjun hip checked Ji-Hun. "Want to know what I'm excited for?"

When Ji-Hun turned to get a read on Seongjun's face, he saw a mischievous smile that told Ji-Hun everything he needed to know.

"How often are we going to be seeing your code word in the group chat?" Ji-Hun rolled his eyes as the mischievous smile turned into a sinister laugh, giving Ji-Hun his answer.

"Hopefully at every stop." Seongjun winked before running to catch up with the rest of the group, leaving Ji-Hun to watch his groupmates, who had become his friends—and after he'd injured his wrist, they had helped him continue to perform as their lead dancer and stay in the group, became his family. This tour was going to be a whirlwind adventure for the six of them, and he felt it.

CLAR1T US tour 시작!

KOREAN VOCABULARY:

막내 – maknae – the youngest in the group

할 거야 – hal goya – I'll do it

이상해 – eesanghae – strange

형 – hyung – older brother, can also be a friendly name from a younger male to an older male

Ji-Hun-아 – Ji-Hunah – an informal, comfortable way to call a friend

시작 – shijak – GO!

CHAPTER ONE

"That can't be a real job," Kat laughed to her friend Dafne as she pushed around bolts of fabric from the rack in the photo studio's prop closet.

"It is!" Dafne exclaimed, pulling out the embroidered lace tulle their boss had been screaming was needed to add the finishing touches to the Victorian-inspired tea set they were photographing.

"A seat filler at an award show? And it pays well?" Kat asked as they exited the closet to make their way back to the set.

Kat needed all the extra cash she could get. While she enjoyed her job working in a photo studio, it wasn't enough to pay both her bills and save for her dream trip to South Korea. She had been taking odd jobs on weekends for the last year for her travel fund, and she was close to reaching her goal. And since Dafne was her best friend, roommate, and future travel buddy, she'd hopped on the odd job train as well. Pooling any extra money they made in a jar in their apartment.

"A thousand bucks for the night."

Korea and *Japan, here we come!*

Kat was internally crunching the numbers as Dafne continued, "And all you do is stand off to the side in the event space and wait for a celebrity to leave their seat. Once they do, you swoop in to fill said seat so that the crowd always looks full."

"How did you even find out about this?" Kat handed the fabric to the set designer, who began to drape the cream tulle with blue and green embroidered flowers across the tea table and chairs.

"I saw it on some TikTok." She shrugged as they stood in front of the computer screens, checking the test shots to see how the fabric was playing with the product and what light needed adjustment. "It had a website. I applied for the two of us. Sent them some photos and they accepted us."

"You sent them photos?" Kat was getting more suspicious of what Dafne had gotten them roped into by the second.

"Calm down." Dafne cooed, holding Kat's upper arm, "It's on the up and up."

It wasn't some sick joke, right? Kat had been fooled more than once before. It was why she had problems trusting people. And it was why she didn't have many friends. Dafne wouldn't do something so fucked up. Kat knew that, but her past still had her on edge.

"Are you in?" Dafne asked, pulling Kat out of her overthinking.

"Fine," Kat responded, knowing she couldn't get out of it even if she tried, "but I'm bringing my pepper spray."

———

KAT WASN'T SURPRISED DAFNE HAD THE CONNECTIONS SHE HAD. The girl could befriend everyone. Hence why she was friends with Kat. Otherwise, Kat would've stayed the quiet, shy girl at the studio. But being next to Dafne, she was at least included in things, even if she still stayed rather awkwardly silent at studio happy hours.

And with Dafne's connections they scored some amazing designer dress samples from an up-and-coming brand she had freelanced for a photo shoot. Emphasis on the *free* part.

Kat admired her friend's flawless beauty. With her tall slender frame, olive skin, long dark brown hair, blue eyes, and plump lips, she was a stunner. She didn't need makeup, her skin naturally glowed. And now that she was in a deep-red floor-length satin gown that had slits up to her hip bones on both sides, and it showed off an ample amount of cleavage, she could probably put some of the celebrities to shame.

It also made Kat self-conscious. Kat willingly hid from the world. After being bullied throughout her school days for her different interests from what was "cool" or "normal," she never felt comfortable around people. And while K-pop and K-dramas were now becoming household interests, back when she was a teen, she was tormented for it, among other things. Even her parents would mock her for listening to things that weren't in English from boys who, according to them, looked like girls. And so she kept quiet, chose to isolate, and made no attempt to find friends in the real world. Her only outlet was online, where she was anonymous and found like-minded people she could fangirl with.

When she got her job at the studio, no one cared what she was into outside of work. She was able to come out of her shell a bit. And when Dafne joined the team and started to stick to Kat's side, she felt she'd found a real safe space and good friend.

"Holy shit, Kat," Dafne squealed and did little taps in her heels as she clipped her earring. "You're fucking hot!"

Kat saw herself in the mirror and wasn't surprised by what Dafne had picked out for her. In fact, Kat knew that, while she felt comfortable in the beautiful mauve satin with long billowy sleeves that tapered at the wrists, Dafne had picked it for the tight-wrapped bodice that made her breasts nearly spill out, the corseted waist taking the place of shapewear, and a singular slit from floor to hip. But Kat wasn't the thin goddess her bestie was.

She was, as one drunk man at a bar had said, "Thicc with two C's."

Dafne had tried to explain it was a compliment and men love women with curves and bodies they can grab onto while enjoying one another, but Kat could only think of the names she was called in high school for having a little extra meat on her bones.

She watched the satin flow softly as she swayed, small hints of her thighs peeking through the slit, and she tried to embrace the sexy. Kat met Dafne's eyes in the mirror, and a caring smile spread across Dafne's face.

"Oh wait! You need jewelry. With a neckline like that, we need to add just a little bit of sparkle to bring even more attention to that amazing rack you have," Dafne hyped as she pulled a double-strand gold necklace from the large accessory organizer hanging on the wall, covered in jewelry for any occasion.

Dafne stood by Kat's side, looking toward the two of them in the mirror.

"Shoes on, and let's go make some celebrity heads turn."

CHAPTER TWO

The job was in fact legit, to Kat's surprise. On more than one occasion, Daf's quick money making opportunities turned out to be scams. They arrived at the music hall along with ten other seat fillers to get their lay of the space. Which was a large auditorium, the stage filled with enormous screens that were testing out the graphics for the awards show. People ran around the stage, setting up microphones as well as testing props and sets for the musical performances. The space in front of the stage, where Kat would be working, was orchestra seating, able to fit hundreds of celebrities, while the balcony would house all the adoring fans. There were names taped all around, reserving specific seats for the different celebrity guests who were coming. They couldn't get a good look at a lot of the names as they were being run around and given instructions on how to act, but Kat assumed it was going to be full of the most popular musicians currently.

The rules were simple. If someone stood up, a runner would fill the seat. One did not talk to the celebrities around them. If they did, they would be escorted out and would not get paid for their time.

"They are not your friends, you are below them," the event manager explained.

After the breakdown of their job, the manager stood them all in line and gave them their designated rows for the seat running. Kat and Dafne got rows right near each other, and they were excited they would be able to hang out together during the breaks when they weren't taking people's seats.

"Alright, people, we have about an hour before they start bringing the guests in, so get to your places. And stay there." The manager clapped and everyone broke away, taking their spots on the sides of the rows.

Kat stood in her area, taking in the architecture she hadn't been able to enjoy while running around getting direction from the team. The ceiling, with its gold filigree borders, was painted like the sky, little angels popping out from the clouds, all looking to the center of the dome where the large globe-like chandelier hung like the sun. The light bouncing off the shimmering crystals had Kat in a trance.

"Looks like one of your K-pop groups is going to be here tonight," Dafne said, pulling Kat from her daze.

"Who? BTS or Stray Kids?" Kat said with a shrug. Not that she wasn't excited to see some of the biggest names in K-pop and, well, pop in general, but she always wished that because of their success, some of the groups she really cared about would get their recognition and be invited to the Western award shows as well.

"Nah. That's old news. I saw them on the list of guests weeks ago." Dafne's face scrunched in confusion as she continued to stare at her phone screen. "Some group name Clar-one-t? Clari… Is this group named after an allergy medication?"

Kat ripped the phone from Dafne's hand to see what she was reading.

@CLAR1T_official: SURPRISE! American CLARvoyants, we are on our way to the Billboard Music Awards! Please support us at our first US award show!

Kat was stunned. CLAR1T was going to be in the same place as her.

"I'm assuming you know who they are?" Dafne joked.

"CLAR1T. They're starting their first US tour this week. I tried to get a ticket, but they sold out in minutes," Kat explained, handing Dafne her phone back, still in a state of shock.

"Well, you might not get to see them perform, but you are about to be in the same building as them."

As Dafne tried to get Kat out of her dream-like state, they saw a production assistant walk over to one of the rows to move around several of the papers for seat designations. And when he walked away, they both looked to the newly rearranged papers.

"I spoke too soon. You won't just be in the same building; you and I will be in the same row as them." Dafne let out a small chuckle. "Let's hope someone sitting next to them has to take a really long piss, or hell, has to leave because of an emergency."

While Dafne joked, Kat was trying not to panic. She didn't want to be that close to an idol group. Never, not once had she ever wanted them to perceive her. Especially not a group she not only fangirled over but read some of the smuttiest fanfictions about. None of that sweet, lovey-dovey fluff that most people like to insert themselves into and dream that one day an idol will fall madly in love with them. No. She read the raunchy "is what they're doing legal?" kind. The kind where you have to take a cold shower to cool off or use your vibrator to get the job done.

Fuck.

———

THE ARTISTS BEGAN TO FUNNEL IN, KAT AND DAFNE STOOD IN THE wings, watching as production assistants led artists to their seats. Kat couldn't take her eyes off all the amazing clothing, trying to keep her mind off the fact CLAR1T, at some point, would be walking down the center aisle to their seats. While Dafne had hoped for the other celebrities around them to leave so they could sit beside them, Kat was praying for the exact opposite.

And as she continued to hope, she was torn from that when loud screams erupted from the balcony, where the fans were seated. And screaming fans usually indicated that someone big had just arrived. When she followed the line of sight from the fans above, she saw the tall figures making their way down the aisle toward her rows.

CLARIT.

"Is that them?" Dafne asked.

"Yep. That's them." Kat couldn't take her eyes off them. She had seen them in their music videos, music show performances, photos, and thirst-trap edits fans made, but it was nothing compared to seeing them in person. Being so close to them left her unable to take her eyes off them. Until another bout of loud screams from the balcony broke her visual to see several other major celebrities making their way to their seats.

"Don't look now but one of your boys is currently undressing you with his eyes," Dafne whispered.

Kat scoffed as she nudged her friend to make it clear Kat thought she was crazy. But when Dafne's eyes continued to stare in the direction of the group, she couldn't stop herself from slowly glancing towards CLARIT, and her eyes met dark ones. Eyes she had seen on her phone, computer, in her dreams, and fantasies. 관지훈. Her ultimate bias.

Fuck, he's even more attractive in person.

She quickly moved her eyes away, taking in his outfit.

His suit jacket, sitting atop his broad shoulders, looked like a soft black velvet. Below the jacket was a shiny, flowing silk top, several buttons undone to showcase a large Cuban link necklace that tightly clung at the bottom of his neck, resting between his protruding collarbone.

As that was all she could see of the outfit, her eyes started to trace back up toward his face. Where heart-shaped lips were cocked to the side in a sexy grin, a slightly wide-based and long-bridged nose, leading her view up to his monolid eyes that seemed to be staring right back at her.

No way was he watching her. His stare wasn't moving. It didn't falter for a second. But Kat's did. She didn't want to be caught by busy bodies and production assistants gawking at the celebrities, potentially losing out on a nice chuck of change for her trip.

"He wouldn't keep eye contact like that if he was watching me," she argued to Dafne. She couldn't stop glancing back, only to catch his eyes dropping down when her lips moved.

"I'm gonna have to disagree." Dafne nudged her. "But there needs to be some way we can confirm or deny because from what I see, he's not only undressed you—in his mind's eye, he's doing a lot more."

"I'll prove he isn't watching me." Kat knew exactly what to do to convince Dafne his eyes were fixated on something behind them. She turned directly toward him, meeting those eyes, and gave a small bow.

And as she came back up, she saw his torso also rising. He had bowed back.

"Holy shit," Kat and Dafne said in unison.

"I was right. He is watching you." Dafne's eyes lit up with amusement.

"Great. He's looking at me. Doesn't mean anything." Kat was trying everything to play it cool, ignore the fact a man she had thought of during some of those cold shower sessions was fixating on her.

"Kat, I don't know whether to slap you or commend you."

"What?"

"You mean to tell me you're going to ignore that man? That man I know you've probably pictured doing some unholy things to you, who is now eyeing you like he shares those same unholy thoughts?" Dafne snapped. "You're not going to make a move on him?"

"One of the only rules we have tonight, Dafne, is to not speak to the artists. We are below them," Kat argued.

"He wants you below him, girl. You're crazy if you don't act on that." Dafne rolled her eyes as she leaned back against the wall.

"And lose out on the thousand bucks they're paying each of us? That could pay for a lot on our trip. I'm trying to think logically."

Kat didn't want to continue having such a ridiculous argument. "I'll skip the flirting and fucking for the money."

"But you admit you want to fuck him?" Dafne jokingly responded, causing them both to laugh and put an end to the conversation.

KOREAN VOCABULARY:
관 지 훈 – Kwan Ji-Hun

CHAPTER THREE

T he event kicked off only a few minutes after Kat had shut down any thoughts Dafne had of 지훈 and Kat getting together in any capacity.

Kat eyed the rows, making sure if there was ever a celebrity getting up, she would be waiting in the wings to take their seat. During one of the performances, she could see some shifting in the seats; someone was making their way out of the aisle. She moved swiftly, and as the audience member left, she snuck in.

She passed all the celebrities, who didn't acknowledge her presence, and found the empty seat. Breathing a sigh of relief, she lifted her head to see who was behind her chair. That relief was short lived when her eyes met the passionate and intense stare from a set of monolid ones.

지훈.

She stood straighter and spun quickly to face the stage, where the musical performance continued. Clapping and swaying like the rest of the people around her, she could feel the burn of his stare on her back. It sent pleasurable shivers up her spine, but her mind quickly fought with her heart.

Kat took several deep breaths, trying to control the ache

forming between her legs as well as the fevered speed of her heartbeat. Why was he studying her so intently? Maybe there was something wrong with her dress? She surveyed her body as she did her little dance to the music. No holes, no stains, the back of the skirt of the dress wasn't tucked into her thong, showing her whole ass.

When the performer finished and everyone started to take their seats once again, she glanced at the end of the aisle, and the celebrity was not waiting to get back in, so she maintained her position, heat still on her neck. She kept her eyes on the stage, hoping the artist would come back to their seat soon.

A finger gently poked her shoulder and instinctively she turned around. The handsome face of the man whose eyes she had been trying to avoid was centimeters away from her. Any closer and their noses would've grazed. She moved her head back, making sure to keep a respectable distance.

"한국 할 줄 아세요?" he whispered, his voice deep, sending vibrations through her body as his minty breath fanned across her face, causing her to shiver. She prayed that he wasn't able to see that reaction. He continued to stare at her, and she realized he had asked her a question.

The rule was not to speak to the celebs. But what was the rule if they spoke to her first? Maybe she could respond without speaking. And so she gave a nod that she understood what he was asking.

He smirked, causing her to clench her thighs together, as he began to mime like a game of charades. He wrapped a hand around his neck, touching his necklace, and her eyes watched his Adam's apple bob.

"아,어...목걸이," he struggled to explain as he pointed between his neck and hers. When she heard 목걸이 she reached up to her necklace, and when she touched it, she felt a pull at the back of her head.

"아," she whimpered from the prick of pain as it tugged her hair. She reached to untangle it, but with every shaky attempt, she could only feel it getting more tangled.

She felt long calloused fingers touch hers, gently forcing her to remove her own fingers. She let her hands drop to her side, and his hands grazed her skin, sending even more heat between her legs. She pushed her thighs tighter than she ever thought possible, giving her any type of friction to alleviate the desire until she was able to get away from him and his delicious touch.

As he pulled delicately, she felt the necklace loosen from its entanglement in her hair, and it gently fell onto her skin. The cool metal shocked her skin. She turned her head only slightly to bow her thanks, trying her best to stay composed.

Her phone vibrated loudly in her dress pocket, causing the celebrities beside her to look over, and she silently apologized as she grabbed her phone to set it on completely silent. In the aisle, she saw the celebrity she had been sitting in for finally had come back. He grimaced when their eyes met; clearly she was taking too long for his liking, but she was thankful to get the hell out of the row. Waiting for the commercial break, she jumped up and ran back out for him to return to his seat.

When she got back to her spot on the wall, she took out her phone to see a text from Dafne.

Dafne: Did I just see the guy previously eye-fucking you now touching you?

Kat swept the rows to see where Dafne had taken up her spot and had to laugh when she saw a well-known artist sneakily trying to read Dafne's phone while she remained blissfully ignorant.

Kat: He was fixing my necklace that was caught in my hair. And look to your left. You've got an admirer. He's been reading over your shoulder for a bit.

She sent a waving emoji and Dafne turned to see the attractive man smile, embarrassed he had been caught. After returning his smile, she flicked her eyes over to Kat to give her a death glare, then back to her phone to type furiously.

Dafne: You're really trying to change the subject? Funny. Not gonna happen. Take a look at your boy. His eyes are STILL on you.

Kat: Whatever, Daf. Nothing is going to come of it so why entertain the idea? He helped me, spoke a bit, and now I can tweet about the amazing kindness CLAR1T

members have for people. I can say I had my Y/N moment.

Dafne: I understood about half of what you just said. You really lost me at the end there.

Kat: What I'm saying is, that's it. I'm not going to say or do anything past that.

"I love you, but you're insane to not make a move on him." The voice of her friend echoed in her head. Wait. No.

She turned to see Dafne stood beside her with a smug smile.

"I'm not insane. You don't understand the power K-pop fans hold," Kat argued.

"Are you not a K-pop fan? And also my best friend?" Dafne countered.

"I mention things in passing to you." Kat glanced up to the balcony to see several cameras pointed at the members of CLARIT. "Look up at the balcony. See those cameras? Those are fansites. Fansites dedicated to singular members of groups. People who would do just about anything to get photos of their bias."

"Bias means favorite, right?" Dafne asked as she watched the balcony.

"Yes. They not only take photos, they record their every move. Some are respectful. They give their idols space and privacy. Others, we call 사생, because they have no sense of privacy and will literally follow these men onto their flights, into their hotels, and even try to get into their vans."

"Jesus." Dafne scoffed as she took another look up to the balcony.

"Yeah. I don't want to be named a 사생, but I also don't want to be attacked by them either." Dafne's eyes widened. "Yes, attacked. To them the idols are theirs. Any kind of relationship, long-term or a one-night deal, if they find the person they are with, expect to be mentally and possibly physically attacked by these 'fans.'"

"Fine. You've proved your point." Dafne put her hands up in defeat.

"Not to mention he could potentially lose his contract if he gets caught seeing anyone," Kat continued.

"Now *that* has to be a joke." Dafne's mouth hung open in shock.

"Nope. It's in most contracts that the idols aren't allowed to date for a certain period of time after they debut. CLAR1T only debuted a year or so ago, so they most likely fall into the 'no dating' category," Kat continued.

"No dating? But they're all insanely attractive. I'm sure people are throwing themselves at them all the time." Dafne faced the line of six men who had their eyes set on the stage. "You're saying those boys actively say no?"

Kat wholeheartedly agreed with Daf. They were all attractive. But they were also incredibly talented. They came from a small company who couldn't afford the big choreographers or music producers, and so they used their own raw talents to put out their first mini album.

But for Kat, it had always been 지훈. He was the group's lead dancer. The one who choreographed most of their performances in the beginning. His voice was also melodic. When one mixed those two together it was a lethal combo. When Kat watched him on the Korean variety shows, or during their vlogs on YouTube, he was always well spoken and seemed very sweet. But when it came to his dancing, she found him overtly sexual and it had, on more than one occasion, made her question just how he used his moves in bed.

"What are you imagining right now?" Dafne's smirk said that Kat had been caught up in her fantasy a little too long. "Your face is—"

She stopped talking, adjusted her dress and pinched her cheeks to give them a stronger rosy tint as she took a step toward a row of seats. Kat was confused until she saw movement from the aisle. Turning, Kat saw 은호, 지훈's groupmate and the leader of the group, making his way out of the row.

His eyes were set on Dafne. A lustful gaze that Dafne seemed totally oblivious to. How could she see someone eyeing up Kat, but have total disregard for the man who was undressing *her* with his eyes as he was making his way over to them?

"Whatever you might plan on saying or doing, don't you dare do it," Kat reprimanded.

"Don't worry. I'm not gonna do anything to ruin your precious group's reputation." Dafne waited for him to exit.

Just as she was about to slide herself into the seat he bowed and said, "화장실이 어디 있어요?"

Dafne's eyes crossed before turning to Kat for translation.

"He asked where the bathroom is," Kat explained, bowing to him as he dipped his head in appreciation.

"Oh, someone out in the lobby should be able to help you find it." Dafne pointed toward the doors as she once again tried to enter the aisle.

He gently grabbed her arm and asked, "Show me?"

Dafne's confusion as he continued to stare, awaiting a response, had Kat covering her smile. For a girl who was so observant of eyes on her friend, she was totally blind to 은호's clear interest in her. Daf said nothing, choosing to give a small nod, and led him out of the auditorium.

Which meant Kat was to be the seat filler. And when she paid more attention, she realized just who 은호 was sitting next to.

Fuck.

KOREAN VOCABULARY:

한국 할 줄 아세요? – hangug hal jul aseyo – Do you speak Korean?

아,어…목걸이 – ah, oh… moggeol-I – ah, umm…necklace

사생 – sasaeng – term for a fan who takes their fanaticism too far. Stalking is among the many problematic things they do.

은호 – Eunho

화장실이 어디 있어요? – hwajangsil-i eodi iss-eoyo? – where is the bathroom?

CHAPTER FOUR

Kat tried to give any of the other seat fillers a chance to take the seat, but they were all preoccupied, and so she slid through the row. While his head didn't move a muscle, his eyes were following her, and her eyes were on him as well. She got to the empty seat and fixed the skirt of her dress to fill the seat beside 지훈. When she was comfortable, she made sure to keep her eyes totally focused on the stage. If she were to glance to her side, she would most likely lose all proper function of her brain and melt into a puddle. His gaze had already made her body hot with desire and plotting out her own fanfiction Y/N story.

She tried to ignore the heat she felt just from his body so close to her side. But it was a fire that only built her desire for the man, and his constant lustful looks throughout the night didn't help.

When is 은호 getting back?

지훈 coughed beside her, causing her to almost jump out of her skin. She did jolt in her seat, turning to finally get a look at him. But it was him who broke the silence between them.

"Are you okay?" His English had gotten much better since the several interviews she had watched on YouTube, and now that English was directed at her.

She was about to respond when she realized if she was caught talking to the talent, she could lose the job and the money for the night. And with that in mind, she nodded.

"Are you sure?" He raised one of his thick black brows. "I saw you with that girl; you can talk, but you won't talk with me," he whispered.

That was harder to answer with a nod or shake of her head. She stared at him, his face expectant of an answer. An answer she was desperately trying to give him without words and hoping he understood.

He nodded, a smirk bringing up the corner of his mouth, and turned away from her. She let out a breath she hadn't realized she had been holding in relief of his understanding.

That relief was short-lived as she felt a tap on her leg and glanced down to see a phone, unlocked, with a message typed out. Eyes wide, she shot her shocked stare up to him and then nervously up and behind them to the balcony.

Turning back to him, she shook her head violently to stop him from trying to talk to her. He rolled his eyes and tapped the phone on her thigh again for her to see the screen.

She read the message:

I have a privacy screen protector. The fansites will not be able to see what is being said. Trust me. You look gorgeous in that dress by the way.

She covered her mouth to hide the small laugh at how he could try to ease her mind and compliment her in so few sentences. When she scanned back up to his face, the smirk he had before was still playing on his lips, but his eyes were focused on her hand covering her mouth.

She alternated the legs she had crossed to fight the friction she was imagining him relieving. But with that, she took the phone from him and responded.

감사합니다. You look very handsome in your suit. Velvet is a great material. Very soft depending on where it was manufactured.

Handing the phone back to him, she realized what an absolute geek about fabric she sounded like and internally scolded herself. *God. Could I be any more awkward? He doesn't fucking care about the feel of velvet!*

She caught in her peripheral 지훈 shimmying to sit taller, and he typed a rather brief message.

Yep. You cockblocked yourself with a stupid comment about velvet. Should've just kept ignoring his glances. Now he realizes what a mistake he made.

He rested his arm on their shared armrest, leaning the phone toward her, and her breath hitched. Her heart felt as if it exploded from her chest.

Want to touch?

She coughed when her breath caught in her throat. In embarrassment and as eyes turned to her, she quickly covered her mouth to muffle the sounds. He moved quickly, reaching below his seat to grab a bottle of water, ripping the cap off, and motioning for her to drink. She bowed her head and took several small sips.

When she finally got the coughing under control, her heart, which had been beating like a hummingbird, had calmed. She felt the warmth of his palm on her back, rubbing and gently patting her bare skin.

She arched her back rapidly to get his touch away from her. *Fuck I'm not going to forget his touch. It's so gentle but his fingers are a bit callous and rough.*

He brought his hand back to his side.

"미안해요," he whispered.

Before she could stop to think what she was doing she responded, "우리 친구들은 어디있죠?"

His eyes went wide, as did hers when she realized she had asked that out loud. She covered her mouth and surveyed the room to make sure the production manager didn't see them talking. 지훈 reached up to pull her hand away from her mouth, his eyes solely focused on her lips. Lips that were gently parted, trying to get any semblance of air into her lungs without sounding like she was having the full-blown panic attack she knew she was going to have.

"목소리가 좋아요. 한국어 발음도 좋아요." He leaned his head closer to her.

No, no. He isn't about to try to kiss me, right?! But why stop him? In fact, she closed her eyes and waited for his lips to touch hers.

But instead of lips on hers, she felt two fingers on her cheek. Her eyes shot open to see he had an eyelash on his thumb. Her eyes met his and a mutual feeling passed between them.

Lust.

She wanted him. Who wouldn't? But the fact that he seemed to also want her was what made it feel like she was in some very vivid dream. She was about say something when a throat cleared at the end of the aisle.

They both turned their attention to Dafne and 은호 waiting for her to leave the seat. Kat refused to turn back toward 지훈 and jumped from the seat to give way to 은호. She bowed toward him as he walked back to his seat, while Kat and Dafne made their way back to the side of the music hall.

"Don't say anything." Kat raised a finger to silence her friend before she could even speak.

But Dafne never knew how to take direction well. "You talked to him, didn't you?" She smirked, clearly already knowing the answer.

Kat rolled her eyes, questioning why she wasted her breath. She peered over toward 지훈, who seemed to be having a similar conversation with his bandmate. His eyes met hers and they both smiled apologetically at one another.

"Here." Dafne's hand blocked her view. In said hand was a small piece of paper with numbers scribbled on it. A foreign phone number was Kat's guess.

"What—"

"It's your boy's phone number. His friend gave it to me. Clearly, he could see your attraction to one another as well." Dafne grabbed Kat's hand to force the number into her palm. "I also may've given his buddy your number. He seems way more open to breaking some little rules."

"They aren't little rules, Dafne," Kat argued. "I'm not about to have him risk his career for a one-night stand."

"He looks willing to risk it. And who said it was going to be a one-night stand?" Dafne argued, nudging her head to 지훈, who was staring at the stage. "If it makes any sort of difference, 은호 said 지훈 noticed you the second they entered the hall and hasn't stopped mentioning you."

Kat cast her glance between her best friend and the idol she had sex dreams about. And every so often at the phone number.

If you do this, you can't back out. Don't be a chicken. If he's willing to break some rules, he must know how not to get caught.

"You want me to live on the edge?" Kat stood straighter, pulled her phone from the secret pocket of her dress, and swiped to a new chat.

But before she could type in his phone number, a new message from an unknown number popped up. The unknown number was the very number scribbled on the piece of paper.

"Holy shit, he isn't playing around. That's him, right? That's his number?" Dafne whisper-screamed at Kat. "What does it say? What does it say?"

"라면 먹고 갈래?" Kat's mind went blank.

"What the hell does that mean?" Dafne questioned.

"Literal translation is 'Do you want to eat ramen with me?', but if your privy to it, it's actually similar to our phrase 'Netflix and Chill.'" Kat couldn't lift her head to see if he was watching. But she could feel his eyes on her.

"He's asking you if you want to hook up?!" Dafne grabbed onto Kat's arm and jumped ever so slightly in her heels.

"Yep."

"Reply, girl." Dafne didn't even give Kat a chance to react before she stole the phone and began typing a message. Kat tried to get the phone back, but they couldn't make a scene, and Dafne used that to her advantage. "You're welcome."

Kat read the message and wished she hadn't.

Kat: Absolutely. Where would you like to go?

"Where would you like to go? Are you insane, Dafne!" She was never going to forgive her.

But then her phone buzzed again.

지훈: 집에 어디야?

Holy shit.

"What's it say?" Dafne was getting excited for the both of them. Kat was freaking the fuck out.

Bzz. Bzz.

지훈: And how about we not tell your friend?

They both shot their heads up to see him covering his laugh. A laugh she had seen countless times on a screen. She had already made the decision to throw caution to the wind, and she was still going to follow through.

Kat: Well we live together, so she does kind of need to know.

"I will be out of your hair. Hell, I packed some junk clothes in a bag so I wouldn't be stuck in this dress all night. I can bum around a coffee shop or something for a few hours."

"I doubt he'll want to spend that much—"

Bzz. Bzz.

지훈: 은호 can take care of your friend.

"Is that Korean for the one who gave me your boy's phone number?" Dafne asked. She sounded as shocked as Kat felt.

Kat nodded, but something bothered her. There was a sick sort of feeling in her chest. He seemed so calm as he was saying such risky things. How many times had he done it before?

But why did she care? He was an idol. Someone she never in a million years would've thought she'd meet, but now he was asking to take her home and fuck her brains out. Maybe it was the fact he was an idol, and she weirdly held him to some higher standard. Which she shouldn't. He was a man, just like any other. A celebrity just like any other. And celebrities had an allure that could get anyone into bed.

"You look unsure…" Dafne brought Kat's attention back to the present, and Kat worriedly stared at Dafne, hoping she would be able to give her the right choice.

"Kat, this is one hundred percent your decision." Dafne grabbed Kat's shoulder. "You can live out your fantasy of having sex with a celebrity. Yours and probably billions of other people's. But I also know you. Hookups aren't your thing. Even if it *is* with a celebrity."

"I—" before she could say anything, they saw someone coming out of a row, and Kat jumped at the opportunity to keep her mind focused on something else for a little while, while she made her choice. And with that, she put her phone into her dress pocket and did everything in her power not to stare at his row until she could make a decision.

KOREAN VOCABULARY:

감사합니다 – kamsahabnida – thank you (formal)

미안해요 – mianhaeyo – sorry

우리 친구들은 어디있죠? – uli chingudeul-eun eodiissjyo? – Where are our friends?

목소리가 좋아요. 한국어 발음도 좋아요. – mogsoliga joh-ayo. hangug-eo bal-eumdo joh-ayo. – I like your voice. Your Korean pronunciation is also good.

라면 먹고 갈래? – lamyeon meoggo gallae? – Want to eat ramyun?

집에 어디야? – neonejib eodiya? – Where is your house?

CHAPTER FIVE

Yes, Kat ghosted 지훈 right in front of 지훈. While she didn't do it intentionally, she believed that it was for the best. Like Dafne had said, Kat wasn't one for meaningless hookups. There was too much history where she didn't realize she *was* a one-night stand. And to add to that justification, she didn't want to be just another notch on an idol's belt.

The award show wrapped up soon after, and the celebrities funneled out rather quickly. That's when Kat and Daf kicked off their heels, feeling the instant relief, and started to walk up and down the aisles to check and make sure nothing was left behind by the guests.

"Everyone!" the production assistant shouted, calling everybody's attention to him. "As a thank you for all your hard work, we ordered several pizzas and have leftover bottles of champagne. Once everything is wrapped up in here, please feel free to come to the foyer and grab some before you leave for the night."

"Oh, free food *and* booze? Say less." Dafne clapped her hands together and began rubbing her palms as she walked the last row and made her way to the foyer.

"I'll be right there. I'm just going to run to the bathroom," Kat hollered as she slipped her heels back on to walk to the toilets.

She pulled open the side door and accidently bumped into a tall, broad-shouldered man who caught her by the waist so she didn't trip in her heels.

"So sorry," she whispered as she glanced up to a familiar pair of eyes, slightly covered by a large black hood from his hoodie. The rest of his face was covered by a mask, but she had seen his face behind masks hundreds of times in airport photos. "지훈?"

"Now you can talk, right?" he said as he pulled down the mask, confirming exactly who she had thought it was.

"What are you doing here?" Kat surveyed the area, making sure no one saw him there and talking to her. She wasn't going to lose out on her pay for the evening.

"Considering you ignored me, in front of me, I thought I deserved an actual response. I'm still racking my brain on how you went from ready to meet up after the show to not even bothering with a response. Was it a little game you like playing?"

"You really shouldn't be here. And to be fair, I didn't send that text confirming, Dafne did." She pushed him to try to get him to leave.

"All I want is understanding, Kathleen," he explained. Her eyes shot up in surprise at hearing her full name. A smirk grew across his lips. "Your friend told 은호 your name for my sake. She also might've mentioned that I'm your bias."

"I'm gonna kill her."

Heat rose on her cheeks, embarrassed at the fact that he knew something that made her sound like the fangirl she was. Luckily, Daf didn't know the term 'ultimate bias,' otherwise the moment would have felt more humiliating for Kat.

As the heat of her blush began to travel the length of her body, a familiar callous hand cupped her cheek. His warmth had her leaning into his touch. She wanted more of it. She could've agreed to anything he wanted in that moment, when she heard loud laughter coming from the lobby.

She moved her face away from his caress to survey the room

around them. She couldn't get him out by way of the lobby, but there had to be a back exit somewhere. And when she turned toward the back exit, she saw Daf and a small group of other seat fillers walking toward the lobby, about to see him and Kat talking.

"Shit." She grabbed his arm and pulled him into the only place she could keep him out of sight for a little while. She pushed through the door, and when she pulled him over the threshold, she slammed the door shut, locking it behind them.

"This is the women's room?" He inspected the size of the space. There was a plush sitting area with multiple couches and chairs across from large mirrors that could be used to freshen up and check their outfits, mostly used for group selfies. Beyond the powder room were the stalls.

"I've heard the rumors about the bathrooms being superior, but this is something else." He tossed his hands in the front pocket of his hoodie as he walked around, taking in all the bathroom had to offer, while Kat was trying to figure out how she was going to get him out of there without getting into trouble.

"Can we stay on task here?" She wasn't in the mood to hear his thoughts on the women's room. She needed to get him out of there unseen. She put her ear to the door to listen for people passing by.

"Sure." He took several long strides over to her and propped a hand beside her head. "Why did you choose not to respond?"

"Because I'm not one for the random hookups. Even if it's you," she blurted out in frustration at being in this situation.

"Who said anything about it being a hookup?" He raised a brow, and she caught his eyes moving down toward her lips.

"Be real, 지훈. Don't try to tell me this isn't your first go at this." She rolled her eyes at the thought that he was trying to convince her he wanted more than her body for a night. "I know exactly what your text meant. As far as I know, it doesn't indicate more than a night."

"I didn't write that text." His eyes came back to hers. "은호 did. Just like your friend responded."

"Maybe they should be the ones hooking up then," she joked, which broke the tension and got them both laughing. As the laughter died down, something else was growing between them. She glanced at his hand on the door, where she could see his veins pulsing as if he was holding himself back from making the move he wanted.

"I'm being honest, Kathleen." He dropped his hand to lean his torso against the door like she was doing. "What if we do this and we realize it could be more?"

"Did that line work on the other women?" She scoffed at how hard he was trying to get her to sleep with him.

"아니," he responded, "I never tried with anyone else."

He chuckled after the admission, which sent a blush covering her whole body again.

"I like when you blush," he flirted. "It doesn't only go across your face, but your chest as well."

He looked down at her bosom, which made her blush even harder. His darkening eyes ignited every nerve ending without laying a finger on her. She clenched her thighs at the wetness pooling between her legs.

"Now you're just teasing me." She decided the only way to keep the damn floodgates from opening was to turn away from him. It helped her avoid his eyes raking over her body and the lust those glances caused.

"Who's teasing who?" His whisper was in her hair, his body curving to her back, his arm wrapping around her waist. She let out a small gasp in surprise when she felt his warm body and hard cock press against her back.

"I'm not," she all but moaned. She knew she should stop him, but his hand that was on her tummy slowly grazed down to the large slit at her thigh. Her mind knew what she had to do, but her body was fighting to stop her from doing it.

His hand brushed the hair away from her neck and she felt his heated breath, causing a shiver of pleasure to roll down her spine.

"We shouldn't," she mumbled, but with the protest, her back arched so that her ass rubbed against his cock.

"You say one thing, but your body says another." His lips were on her shoulder. Soft and warm. She wanted more. She wanted those lips on her own.

"한 번만," she blurted out. Even her mind had given up the good fight. At least this time she knew what she was getting herself into. Unlike some of her previous occasions.

"네?" His hand at the slit of her dress paused. As if he was in a state of surprise she was offering to him what he was begging to have.

She turned around in his hold to make sure when she spoke, what she was saying was loud and clear. "We do this one time. Get it out of our systems, delete each other's numbers, and call it quits. I have a fun story to tell my grandkids, and you can add me to the list of fangirls you've slept with."

"Kathle—"

"Also don't call me that. It's Kat. Only my mother calls me Kathleen, and only when she's angry." Kat arched back to get a better look at his face, and it was an expression she had never seen on him before. His bottom lip hung open, his eyes were solely focused on her lips as she spoke. And when she had finished talking his tongue came out to pull his bottom lip between his teeth.

"고양이," he whispered, leaning down to graze his nose against hers, but she grabbed the sides of his chin, squeezing his cheeks together, making his lips pucker.

"Call me *that* again and you won't be able to dance ever again." She gave his face one more squeeze before letting it go and pushing his head back a bit.

He grabbed her wrist with the sexiest smile she'd thought she would only see in a fancam or one of those eye contact challenge videos as he brought her wrist to his lips. His kiss was sweet and soft. The pressure was delicate, and if she hadn't seen his lips on her skin she would've questioned if it happened. The way her stomach flipped and her heartbeat skyrocketed to an alarming pace, her body confirmed it.

"I like this feisty side of you. Much more fun than you trying not to talk to me." His breath tickled her wrist, causing her to shiver in his embrace, and his arm squeezed around her waist. His lips kissed her palm, his ever-darkening eyes focused on hers.

He took a step closer, making her stumble back. Followed by another and another until she felt something on the back of her knees. She turned her head to see he had walked them to the couch.

"What are you—"

"Touch yourself." He cut her off with his command.

"네?" She was suddenly happy he had walked them over to the couch, because she needed to sit down after hearing him say something she had read in some of the thousands of fan fictions she'd devoured. He crouched down in front of her, his hand still holding her wrist. That's when she noticed the scar on his wrist. She remembered he sustained an injury almost immediately after CLARIT debuted. The company said it wasn't that serious, but seeing the scar made her question how severe it might've been.

He turned his attention to her hand and with a grin, brought her fingers closer to his mouth. She expected him to kiss them like he had her palm, but instead he took two of her fingers in his mouth and swirled his tongue around them before pulling them out with a small popping noise.

"I want you," he began, "to touch yourself."

His eyes then lingered from her fingers that had just been in his mouth to the slit of her dress before finishing his statement, "With these two fingers."

"I've never—"

"Masturbated?" he cut her off with an inquisitive brow and a growing smirk.

"That's not it. I've masturbated, just not in front of someone." The blush he'd declared he enjoyed covered her cheeks and chest as she admitted that to him.

"Well then, the men you've been with are not only boring partners, but they also never cared to take the time to find what *you* enjoy." He grabbed the hem on the slit of her dress and gently pulled it aside to flaunt her bare thighs, the dimples and all. She shivered not just from the cool air touching her newly revealed skin, but also from the way he licked his lips as his eyes raked over every inch of her.

"달콤한 냄새야." He took a deep inhale, which made her clench her legs tighter to hide the arousal he clearly could smell.

He brought her fingers back to his mouth, wetting them again as she thought about what he had said. He wasn't wrong. The past few partners she had, the guys were done quick, focusing solely on themselves and their pleasure and never hers. When they would fall asleep, she would usually sneak off into the bathroom to get the job done herself.

The irony of her current situation wasn't lost on her.

His warm hand cupped her cheek as he said, "Come back to me, 우리 애기."

"What did you call me?" she breathed out, as she wasn't sure her voice would be able to handle much more.

"우리 애기. At least for tonight." He leaned forward and brought his lips to hers.

It was electrifying. His lips were more than she had ever imagined. She wanted to memorize the soft pressure he was using. It expressed yearning for her to give in to him. Every part of her body tingled as heat built throughout. Her thighs, which had been clenching together to relieve her ache, released slowly to get what she really desired.

He pulled his lips away, causing her to lean forward to maintain the connection. When she opened her eyes, she saw her lipstick smeared on his lips, and she tried to bring her hand to wipe it away but realized it was still in his grasp.

"Spread your legs more for me," he commanded. She quickly opened them, a sexy grin growing on his lipstick-stained lips, and she could've sworn she heard him say, "Attagirl." His eyes went down to her chest. "Your tits look amazing in this dress."

Reading the vulgar words in a fan fiction were nothing compared to hearing them being directed at her. She let out an involuntarily moan at his rough words. He brought his lips to her chest, her breasts precariously held in the dress, and left hot open-mouth kisses on every inch he could. His tongue swiping before his lips descended to suck gently.

"Perks of being fat," she moaned as she leaned forward to allow him better access to her chest, but his lips stopped.

"If you're trying to minimize your beauty, I don't find that statement funny." He leaned back on the heels of his shoes.

"I wasn't——" She stopped herself. He wasn't totally wrong. For most of her formative years, she was deemed the overweight, weird fangirl who had no friends. She began to hate walking past mirrors, and if she did, she would end up pointing out all her flaws. After befriending Dafne, things had changed somewhat. She'd learned to love more of herself, and she'd come to accept that fat doesn't mean ugly, but there were still moments where she couldn't feel confident, and the world did try to knock her down a peg.

Especially when it came to someone finding her desirable. She always questioned compliments and the intentions behind them.

"I lost you in your thoughts again." 지훈's soft and sultry voice brought her back into the moment.

"미안, I just…" She wasn't able to explain what she was feeling.

"Don't apologize. You're cute when your mind wanders." His fingers began to trace her breasts, causing her to close her eyes and lean closer to his warmth.

"You're right," she blurted out. His touch had a magic power that caused her to give in to anything he wanted.

"That you're cute?" he chuckled.

"아니." She shook her head and opened her eyes to see she had leaned so far forward their faces were a breath away from one another. Her eyes met his. "You're right that I was being self-deprecating."

His smile turned to a frown—was his expression understanding?

"I'm sorry you feel that way about yourself." His hand finally dropped its hold on her wrist, sending her body into a panic. Had she said something to ruin the mood? But both his hands moved to her waist, digging into her bouncy flesh, and pulled her to the edge of the couch, spreading her legs as wide as she could to allow him to fit in between.

"Because from the second I laid my eyes on you, they never wanted to leave. You're stunning." The hungered desire in his voice, his breath touching her chest, had her nipples harden against the soft fabric of her dress, which only heightened their sensitivity. Her body was on fire under his gaze. She smiled softly.

"And that smile?" He brought one of his hands back up to her cheek, his thumb caressing her lips before pulling the bottom one down a bit. "All I thought about was how I could get it directed at me."

Her smile grew as she leaned her cheek into his hold. "Is it weird to say that I feel the sincerity of your statement?"

"Well, you should feel it. I'm being one hundred percent honest." He smiled back. "And since I'm being so honest, let's get back on topic. I want to watch you finger fuck yourself before I take over and make you cum several times on both my mouth and cock."

"Jesus." She exhaled at how dirty his words were and how much they turned her on. Words she could never imagine an idol saying. And it was her ultimate bias saying the lust-inducing words directly to her.

His one hand left her waist to again to grab her hand and bring her fingers to his mouth. His tongue swiped at them, slid between them, and all she could imagine was him doing that between her legs. She let out a small squeak as he took them out and maneuvered her hand close to her wet center.

"Don't be scared," he whispered as he sat up on his knees to place a gentle kiss on her lips as he directed her fingers to graze herself, eliciting a moan. "씨발, I wanna hear so many more of those."

His hand dropped hers to let her begin her own ministrations as he let his hands roam the rest of her body. Touching every ounce of skin with feather-light touches. She was getting so distracted by him and what he was doing to her that she wasn't thinking about what he had asked of her to do to herself.

"How about we remove this? Give you better access to yourself." He hooked his index finger around the elastic of her thong, most definitely feeling how wet she was, and he pulled hard. It wasn't the tug that surprised her, it was the snap and sting against her pussy that had her grab onto his shoulder and bite her bottom lip.

"야…" he trailed off with a groan, his eyes meeting hers. "Don't hold back your moans. I want to hear them all. Every." He grabbed her hand to bring her fingers back to his mouth. "Last." He sucked them, coating them with his saliva. "One."

He brought her fingers back down to her center and instructed, "Play with yourself, 우리 애기."

He dropped down, almost sitting on the floor, his eyes focusing between her legs. "I want to watch you bring yourself close to the edge, and then let me help finish."

She took the first swipe at herself, and her body fell back onto the couch. Her fingers circled her clit, her hips grinding to get more of the friction she willingly gave herself. She closed her eyes, nervous to see what his expressions were. Was he disgusted? Was he turned on? She very much thought it could be the latter, but she didn't want to be disappointed if, when she looked down, she saw him holding back a laugh.

He wouldn't do that, her mind argued.

I don't even know him, she fought back against her mind.

After circling her clit a few more times, she gave a light press before letting two fingers slip easily inside herself. She arched her back, letting out a soft moan.

"씨발," she heard him groan, followed by a deep exhale. At that she couldn't stop herself from opening her eyes to see his reaction. And her heart fluttered, her stomach formed massive knots when she saw his mouth hung open, his cheeks flush, his hand running through his hair, and eyes watching her fingers like her ministrations were that of a maestro.

No man had watched her with such a hunger. It sent stronger waves of bliss up and down her spine, her body tingled, and she pumped her fingers harder into herself.

"Don't you want to—" she pressed on her clit with her thumb, causing her to choke on her own words.

"뭐가?" He sat up straighter.

"Touch?" she finished her previous sentence, knowing she wasn't going to be able to ask it in full again. She had found a rhythm, quicker than her usual, and was losing focus on everything around her.

"Is that what you want, 우리 애기?" That devilish smirk appeared on his face again, and if he had kept it on his face any longer, she would've cum right then. She closed her eyes, focusing on her rhythm. That was until a third finger, that she knew was not her own, plunged inside of her, reaching farther than any of her fingers ever could.

"I want to feel you cum around at least one of my fingers," he breathed, leaning over their hands to get closer to her face, which was too far away in their position, "for now."

But his face was perfectly situated at her chest. His hand that wasn't inside her cupped one of her breasts, and even with how big his hand was, her tits were bigger and spilled over. He pulled at the fabric and her breast fell completely out. She was about to stop him. Her nerves again afraid that if he saw her naked body, he would be turned off, but a feral growl came from him as his mouth descended on her breast.

"Even better than I imagined," he murmured. His lips tripped on her skin before taking her nipple into his mouth and sucking hard while she pressed onto her clit, causing her to arch her back, her breast nearly covering his face from her point of view.

He pulled back only to grab the fabric covering her other breast and reveal her entire chest to him, and his fingers began to play with one nipple while his mouth mimicked on the other.

It was sensory overload. She couldn't catch her breath. Every pump of their fingers, every nip and suck of his mouth on her breasts had her approaching her high.

"That's it," he egged her on, "Let me hear all the sounds you can make."

Their fingers were pumping at a brutal pace, his curving to hit that perfect spot, making her moans impossible to control.

"I can feel you clenching around our fingers. You're ready. Cum for me." He whispered before biting down on her nipple and pressing his thumb to her clit.

The orgasm ripped through her. She didn't see stars. She saw pitch black. She had never felt an orgasm rock through her body like that. Never came so hard that she had no clue where she was, who she was with, hell, she even forgot her own name for a second.

When her sight started to come back, she glanced down to see her hand gripping 지훈's hair and his face pressed to her chest.

"어머, 미안." She released his hair and his mouth left her breast with a soft pop.

"하지마," he said as he slowly, torturously slowly, pulled his finger out of her. "Don't apologize for enjoying yourself."

He brought his finger up to reveal its wetness. That was *her* coating his finger. She searched around to find something they could use to wipe it when she noticed he was bringing his finger toward her mouth.

"입 열어봐." He dropped his jaw to mimic what he wanted her to do. She followed immediately and his finger entered her mouth. She closed her lips around it, taking in her own flavor. He reached between them to grab her hand that still sat between her legs, pulled them out gently and brought them to his mouth.

Holy fuck. This was never in the fan fictions. This is fucking hot.

His tongue parted her fingers sucking and licking every bit of her pleasure. Their eyes met and didn't part until he pushed his finger further into her mouth and down her throat, causing her to gag and cough.

"미안." He pulled all fingers out to apologize.

That apology triggered an awkwardness between them, and she closed her legs, pushing him away from her. He stumbled and sat on the floor, while she pushed her breasts back into the dress and covered her legs.

"We should probably get out of here." She tried to stand, her legs feeling like jelly so that she moved a bit slower.

"And where should we go?" He stood and towered over her.

Fuck, if I wasn't worried, I'd squish him, I would climb him like a tree.

"What time do you need to be back?" she asked.

"Tomorrow morning." He grabbed at the fabric of her skirt.

"Won't you be in trouble?" She wasn't sure what she should do with her hands, and they began to fiddle with each other.

"Nope. We have code words to cover up whenever we do things we're not supposed to. In case the manager asks where we are." He dropped her skirt to brush his hair back as he pulled his hood up, and she could swear his jawline got sharper.

"Oh?" She was learning more than she could've ever dreamed of as a fangirl. Things only she would know. Well, not only she would know. With what just transpired between them, it couldn't have been his first time doing this. She needed to stop getting her hopes up where they shouldn't be.

"We'll tell the other members we are grabbing something to eat." He reached into his sweatpants to adjust himself, which had her wondering why he hadn't made his move to get himself off. "When they ask what, we give our special code food and they know what they have to do."

"And your food is?" she asked, her eyes moving from his package to his face.

"That depends on if, when we walk out of here, we're walking out together or separate." He reached out for her hand.

Could she do it? Technically they hadn't done the "one time" she had put on the table, and he clearly still wanted to spend more time with her. But could her mind fully separate the fan fiction idol she had built in her head, from the real deal idol who was standing right in front of her?

She cast her eyes down at his open hand and let her heart make the decision. Her heart chose to place her hand in his. He wove their fingers together and brought the back of her hand to his lips for a soft kiss.

"I do owe you an orgasm." She was trying to play it cool like her heart wasn't about to jump out of her chest and thank her for letting it decide for once.

"And I owe you about six." He laughed as he pulled her close to lay a gentle kiss on her lips.

His laugh continued after the kiss and was so brilliant in the way it showed his white teeth and caused his cheeks to scrunch, reminding her of a cute little chipmunk. It was contagious, infectious, and she began to laugh along.

"This is a yes?" he asked, confirming.

His free hand was on the lock of the door, waiting for her answer.

"네."

Korean Vocabulary:

아니 – ani – no

한 번만 – han bonman – only once

네? – nae? – literally is "yes?" But the term phrase can be used many different ways. This time it is being used as "What?"

고양이 – goyang-i – cat

달콤한 냄새야 – dalkomhan naemsaeya– you smell sweet/delicious

우리 애기 – uri aegi – literal translation is "our baby." In Korean they don't use "I" or "me" because they consider it egocentric.

미안 – mian – sorry (informal)

씨발 – ssibal – fuck

야 – ya – this is another phrase that can be used in many different ways. In this instance it's in a pleased "wow" way.

뭐가? - mwoga? – do what?

어머 – eomeo – OMG

하지마 – hajima – stop it

입 열어봐 – ib yeol-eobwa – open your mouth

CHAPTER SIX

지훈's blood was rushing more powerfully to his dick. Kat had given the full send on, letting him have her for the rest of the night. And he planned to have her in every which way he could.

The second he had laid eyes on her at the show, he was stunned by her breathtaking smile when she laughed with her friend. No woman, in the crowds of thousands at their concerts, had rendered him speechless. Never.

When she sat down in front of him, the desperation to speak with her was so obvious that 은호 nudged him to make an attempt. And fuck, when he felt her heated skin against his fingers as he helped her fix her necklace, all he could imagine was marking her skin, making her his. And the way her body reacted to his touch was heaven on Earth. He wanted her. And he was going to have her.

But then she had ignored his text about where to meet to hook up. In all fairness, 은호 and her friend were the ones who initiated the idea of meeting up. He thought he had misinterpreted Kat's reactions to his touch. That maybe her shivers weren't of pleasure but of disgust.

After he left the venue, he couldn't get her out of his head. He had been turned down before, but this one bothered him more than any other. He enjoyed the surprise on her face when she saw who she had bumped into, but not as much as he enjoyed watching the ecstasy as she fingered herself. But then joining in to make her cum? He almost came in his pants at the feeling of her riding his finger with his head between her breasts. He wanted to see all the different kinds of reactions he could get. And if he only had one night to get them, he wasn't going to waste any more time.

He unlocked the door, grabbing her hand to pull them out and sneak past the people who still were lingering to enjoy the free food and champagne.

Was it this dark when I got here?

"Why is it so dark?" She surprised him by asking exactly what he was thinking, her hand squeezing his.

Before he could respond, they received a hint that something wasn't right. The lobby was completely empty. Not a sound other than their own footsteps. And as he went to push the front door to exit, they got their answer. The door didn't budge.

"아이 씨—" He pushed again.

"Are we—" She let go of his hand to try another door, getting the same result.

"네, we're locked in." He pushed the hood off his head and ran his fingers through his hair as he tried to figure a way out.

"I'm sure there is another exit. It's a fire hazard to not be able to get out," she argued.

"Not without sounding an alarm," he rationalized. "Alarms bring attention."

"We can make a run for it," she tried to reason.

"You can barely walk in those heels right now, you want to take them off and run barefoot on the streets of LA?" He raised a brow.

He watched as her shoulders slouched for a second but shot right back up as if a light bulb went off. She patted down her dress, reaching into the pocket on her hip and pulled out a phone. *Brilliant.* He smiled hopefully before her face drooped and her head dropped.

"Dead." She showed him the black screen. "What about yours?"

"Didn't bring it." He shrugged.

"뭐?" Her eyes were wide as her bottom lip dropped, leaving that mouth he wanted to devour wide open.

"Once I give my group members my code phrase, I leave my phone in my room," He explained. "That way, if down the road our manager wants to check our locations, he could see I was where I was supposed to be."

"Does your manager actually do that?" The shock on her face was cute.

"No, but we can never be too careful when it comes to our private lives." He shrugged. His thought process might sound illogical to some, but to his groupmates and other idols, it was just the way of their world.

"Okay, so we only have one phone and it's dead, and we can't open a door because an alarm will garner attention you don't want…" She began looking around. And quickly spun back to him with a raised brow and one index finger in the air.

"This is a theater, right?" she asked.

He nodded. And she continued, "Well, that means there is a backstage, with a greenroom or dressing rooms. I'm sure there are probably phone chargers in one of the rooms."

He was happy someone knew how to problem-solve in a panic. He put out his hand for her to take once again, enjoying the warmth her hand gave him. It wasn't only a literal feeling, but also a sense of comfort and trust he didn't feel often with people outside his small group. He liked the way her warmth spread through his whole body, leaving him in a state of emotional euphoria. Added to the euphoria was also the depraved thoughts of what he wanted to do to her once they got out of the theater.

Once backstage, he tried to turn several door handles, but they were locked. He was about to lose hope when he finally heard the click of one opening. When he pushed the door open, it wasn't a dressing room, but a prop room. There were wigs lined on several shelves near glassware, books, vases, and racks of clothing. At the very back of the room he saw a desk. Most likely there would be a charger there.

Her hand squeezed his, and when he turned to see her, he caught a glint of fear in her eyes. "괜찮아."

When they got to the desk, he was happy to have been correct. There, plugged into an outlet, was a long charging cable.

"Oh, thank God." She dropped his hand and ran to plug in her phone. "Dafne will get us out of here."

While she waited for her phone to turn on, he took to roaming the room to admire the props and costumes neatly organized and categorized.

It was like his own tour, but on a much grander scale. CLARIT had only just debuted, and while their international success was flourishing, in Korea, they were still a mid-tier group, from a mid-tier company, with a mid-tier budget. They were still all roommates in a small dorm where it was three to a room. Not much for privacy, let alone a collection of clothing and other memorabilia.

He was trying to keep his mind off his constant questioning of if he had made the right life choice when he heard Dafne right behind him ask, "So this is what you see on a regular basis?"

"Not at this scale." He turned to face her. He brushed against her breasts as he turned, his mind going back to when his face was pressed between them, causing his already rock-hard dick to become painfully more erect.

"This reminds me of the prop room in our office." She smiled as her hand grabbed at some of the fabric. "Minus the bits of clothing. We do accessories, home décor, and basically anything but clothing. Dafne loves clothing photography though. She freelances on weekends. It's how we got these dresses." She pulled at the skirt, revealing to him her soft milky legs that he wanted to be crushed between. "She wants to style people, not things."

Her face changed when she talked about Dafne. Her smile was soft, her eyes crinkled in the corners, and her brows relaxed. Her whole body was more at ease. Clearly Dafne was special to her.

"You care about her a lot," he posited.

"She's my best friend. Of course I do." She laughed. "She's my only real friend in all honesty. I was bullied through most of my formative years. I was told no one would love me, care for or about me." She sighed, as if the story was normal and old news. Walking away from him, she made her way down an aisle, but he followed her. To their shock, they found a twin bed.

They looked at each other and then back toward the bed. With a simultaneous shrug they made their way over and sat down.

"After all those comments, I shut down and shut out most people. If anyone had something nice to say, all I could think was that it was a joke." She choked up with sadness.

Hearing her choke made him reach out to grab her hand. "Kat—"

"But Dafne wouldn't stop being so damn kind." Kat's head fell back with a laugh. He assumed it was to keep the tears from falling. "She kept talking to me at work, and then one day she asked me if I wanted to move in with her because her roommate bailed. But—"

"You thought it was a joke." He finished the sentence for her, his own eyes stinging with tears as he thought of this beautiful woman not seeing just how breathtaking she was on the outside. And as he continued to learn more about her, he was seeing just how beautiful she was on the inside as well.

"It took almost a month for her to convince me to even look at the place. And that was only because she was having a party with a bunch of our coworkers. I was nervous as hell walking into that party." Her laugh held a deep sadness that he wanted to take away.

"And there was Dafne, screaming with the brightest smile as she saw me walk in the door, and pulling me around the apartment to show me all the space and finally the empty room she was desperately trying to fill."

His hand reached over to cup her cheek and bring her face toward him.

"She's helped me come out of my scared shell bit by bit." A tear she had been trying to hold back hit his thumb, and he gently brushed it away.

"Remind me to thank her." He smiled gently because he genuinely meant his statement. He wanted to give Dafne a medal.

"Why would you thank her?" she asked as she wiped the tears out of her eyes before more fell. It just made more fall and land on his hand, which was swiping at her cheek to stop them from running all the way down her face.

"Would you have been here, at the award show, dressed in this gorgeous dress that caused me to stop breathing when I saw you in it, if it weren't for her?" His smile grew into an all-out grin at her eyes widening and a small hiccup jostling her breasts.

"This dress is so fucking uncomfortable." She shimmied, making the bed bounce.

"Dodging the question?" he joked.

"I wasn't. You're right. I wouldn't be here. And I definitely wouldn't be locked in here with my ult bias if it—" She stopped and turned her head away from him, his hand falling from her face. It was too late. He knew what he'd heard, and the smile that was already wide began to hurt with how happy hearing that little slipup made him.

"Ult bias? I'm your end all and be all?" He grabbed at her hands as she tried to shimmy away from him, but he wasn't going to let her. He watched as her chest started to go that lovely shade of red he was desperate to see all over her body.

"미안해, that is so embarrassing. I can't believe I said that out loud." She tried to cover her face, but he was not going to let her.

"I need to make sure I stay your ultimate bias." He moved closer, his side pressed to hers as he leaned his face as close as he could get without touching her. "No one is ever going to take my place."

His lips descended onto hers and the hunger he had been keeping at bay since seeing her in the bathroom had broken through and consumed him. Her lips were still as sweet as candy, and his tongue licked to have a taste but was met with the salt of her tears. She opened her mouth to let out a moan, but he captured it in his own.

"I want to make love to you so you'll never forget how beautiful and desirable you are." His lips traced down her neck, her head dropping back to give him all the access he wanted. His hands started to roam her body, but he was getting annoyed at the bodice of the dress. He wanted to feel her skin. All of it.

"일어나기," he groaned out his command.

"네?" she whispered breathlessly.

"Get up and turn around." He nipped at her chest, leaving a small mark, and with a growl he thought about how many more he wanted to leave on her.

She stood up and turned around, facing the bed. Her gorgeous plump ass was at eye level. He stood and walked up behind her. She turned her head to the side to look at him as she asked, "이렇게?"

He caught her thighs rubbing together and wanted to feel how wet she was for him.

"좋다." He stared at the zipper that would release her whole body to him. His fingers played along the bare skin of her upper back before taking hold of the zipper, and with a gentle tug, it began to drop and reveal more of her skin. He noticed her body tensing.

"You said this dress was uncomfortable." He put his lips to her neck, kissing down to her shoulder. "I'm helping you get comfortable."

He pulled the zipper a bit more, her body relaxing with its freedom, but her arms came up to hold the front up, hiding the chest he desperately wanted free.

"I want you naked in front of me, 애기," he whispered in her ear. Which he saw made her clutch the front of the dress even tighter. He took a step back. She wasn't comfortable with him, and he wasn't about to push her into something that could make her regret not only enjoying a night together, but keeping him as her ultimate bias.

"미안," she whispered. "I'm just really nervous. I don't do this kinda thing. Obviously." She laughed as she faced him, still holding the dress against her chest.

"Why obviously?" he questioned.

"I told you about how people said I could never be loved." She sat back down on the bed. "Well, my short list of 'romantic' encounters have added to the notion I'm also shit at sex." She dropped her head and wiped at her cheeks. He took a step closer to her. "Fuck, now I'm crying about being bad at sex in front of you. Can I be any more embarrassing?" She rolled her eyes as the tears continued to fall.

"First off, I doubt you're the one who is bad at sex. Most men are cocky assholes who think it could *never* be their fault." He grabbed her shoulders, trying to ignore how delicately soft they felt. Like silk against his fingers. "I just watched you cum so hard with only a little help from one of my fingers. I can guarantee you, *you* are *not* the problem." He put his hand under her chin to lift her head. He wanted to find every single person who'd made her feel less than the beautiful woman she was and make them apologize, which would then be followed by him punching them in the dick to make sure they felt a fraction of the pain they caused her.

"Secondly, as your ult bias, I'm here to remind you of how stunning you are inside and out. I can't have a CLARvoyant as amazing as you think anything different." He smiled his brightest, cheesiest smile, which got her to laugh, and through the tears he saw her radiance shining again.

"You sure know how to woo a girl. Is it all part of your plan to get a different girl at each stop of the tour?" she tried to joke, but he could tell she was probing to see if that really was his intention.

"씨발. 너무 아름다워." He couldn't control his thoughts at that point.

"Avoiding the question?" She played the same card he had only a few minutes earlier.

"아니. I just didn't like the question." He pinched her chin softly before sitting beside her again. "I already told you how I couldn't take my eyes off you during the ceremony. I wanted you then. I want you now. And I understand your nervousness about what we're doing. It's one night. With the tour, the no dating rule, the literal world between us, this night might be all we have."

He dropped his head, worried he had just screwed up everything, but he didn't want her to think he was forcing her to do anything she didn't want to. He felt the bed bounce and lift slightly.

"Well then…" she said as her heeled feet moved between his legs. And then a puddle of satin covered her feet, followed by a thong. His eyes darted up to every delicious piece of her body on display in front of him. "Let's make this night count."

Korean Vocabulary:

아이씨 – aissi – this is a phrase of frustration. Similar to our "damn".

네 – nae – yes. This instance is the literal use of the word.

뭐? – mwo? – What?

괜찮아 – gwaenchanh-a – it's okay

미안해 – mianhae – sorry (informal)

일어나기 – il-eonagi – stand up

이렇게? – ileohge? – like this?

좋다 – johda – good

너무 아름다워 – neomu aleumdawo – so beautiful

CHAPTER SEVEN

K at was terrified. And shockingly it had nothing to do with the fact that she was totally naked in front of 지훈, her ultimate bias, but more so because she had a very limited knowledge of real-life experience when it came to sex. Insanely erotic fan fictions where one of the characters were tied up, or they were using all sorts of different items to help each other get off, was interesting to read, but when it came to actual practice, all she could say she'd tried was missionary and had given a few blowjobs.

He grabbed the meat of her hips and pulled her closer to him. She stumbled a bit, still in her heels with the dress and panties at her ankles.

"Straddle me," he commanded.

"But—" She was nervously about to mention her weight again but was cut off by him kissing her tummy. From one side to the other, he laid hot open kisses all over her stomach, his hands gripping her hips harder. His tongue slid down, tripping into her belly button. She watched in shock and awe at how he was worshiping all of her.

"Get on top of me right now. I hate having to repeat myself, 애기." His voice had gotten so much deeper. A tone she had never heard in the countless interviews she had watched, or all the songs she had listened to. She wondered how many people had heard that lust-filled, sultry tone.

She obeyed him, stepping out of the dress and thong, and he leaned forward, his lips on her tummy as he picked them up and tossed them to the side. One leg on the outside of one of his thighs, the bed squeaked as all her weight came down on the one knee, and she lifted the other to the outside of his other thigh. Her own inner thigh muscles were screaming a bit at the new position, so she sat up a little to let them ease into their arrangement.

His hands moved from her body to his own, pulling off his hoodie to reveal his bare chest. He was more muscular than most other idols she liked. But she could add that to the reasons he was her ult. She always joked he would be the type to carry his woman. Whether a piggyback when she's too drunk to walk, bridal style if she got injured, or over his shoulder as he playfully carried her to their bedroom.

Her hands reached out to explore, and the second she touched him he exhaled deeply and nodded for her to continue. When she leaned farther back, sitting more comfortably, she gave herself a better view of his whole naked torso, which caused her to pause when she noticed something dark on the side of his ribcage.

"That tattoo in your last music video…" Her fingers trailed over to the black ink that painted a large portion of his ribs.

He grabbed her hand, and when she focused on his face, she could see panic in his eyes.

"You can't tell anyone," he blurted. His breathing had become shallow.

"An hourglass?" she asked.

"Kat, seriously you can't—"

"I'm not going to tell anyone, 지훈." She pulled her arm from his grip, which wasn't tight to begin with and brought her hand back down to trace around the tattoo. "Why an hourglass?"

He took a deep breath in what she assumed was a nervous but trusting manner. Nervous to open up, but trusting she wouldn't tell anyone what she learned.

"Many things." He leaned back on his hands, allowing her more access to his torso to trace whatever pattern she wanted on his six pack, but she was solely focused on the tattoo. "Time heals, don't waste a second, live like it's your last day, and so on. It has so many meanings to me."

"I like that." She smiled, their eyes meeting. Her fingers finally moved from the tattoo, making their way to the waistband of his sweatpants. "Let's not waste another second."

She tugged the elastic, which caused him to lift his hips. His hard cock, still sheathed in his sweats, ground up to finally meet her wet center, and she desperately wanted to grind down, but she wanted to feel him bare and rubbing against her. She pulled the pants a bit farther and that's when his hand went between them to help remove the offensive clothing.

"애기," he moaned, his hand moving from in between them but not before taking a swipe at her drenched core, making her meet his moan with one of her own. But two could play that game, and she reached down, finally feeling the soft smooth skin of his hard cock. It was bigger than she anticipated. She wrapped her hand around and gave a gentle tug that made his head fall back.

"Fuck, Kat, I need to be inside you," he begged, his hands gripping her hips, and he again ground up to meet her. His tip probed at her entrance, but he paused. "I don't have a condom. I didn't think—"

"I'm on the pill. And I'm clean, had a check a while back. And I haven't been with anyone in, well, more time than I want to admit." She blushed and tried to hide her embarrassment, but 지훈's hand cupped her cheek.

"That rosy blush of yours"—his hand traveled from her cheek, along her neck, across her chest, tripped over one of her hardened nipples, down her tummy, and onto her thigh—"really does cover your whole body."

"지훈," she moaned as his hand traced her inner thigh, making its way to where she was ready to take him.

"네 애기?" He sat up, his lips brushing her neck but never fully landing. His breath sending shivers rocking through her as his fingers slid through her folds and found her clit in an instant. Her grip on his dick followed his motion, sliding through her folds and rubbing the head of his cock, almost letting him slip inside her.

"I—" She choked as his finger pressed on her clit, causing her to use her free hand to grab his shoulder to keep her balance.

"Use your words," he whispered into her ear before biting down on her lobe.

"I want you…" She needed a second to catch her breath before finishing, "to fuck me."

"Oh, 애기." His lips connected with her cheek and then softly brushed her lips. "I'm not going to fuck you."

She leaned away from him, thinking he was playing a sick joke. His eyes shimmered with amusement. Was she getting played?

"You've been getting fucked by all those losers in the past." He kissed her neck. "I want to show you what it's like to *have* someone. To be *taken* by someone and receive all the pleasure you deserve." His lips moved down from her neck and throat to her chest. She dropped her head back as his tongue traced her shoulders.

"Right now, you're going to ride this cock however you want." His hot, wet kisses landed on her nipple, giving it a flick of his tongue before he continued, "You're going to cum multiple times. And then we're going to explore even more positions that make you scream and moan in pleasure." His mouth moved to her other breast to repeat what he had done and make both her nipples pebble. "Tonight, you're going to see how good you can feel being with someone who focuses on you."

His hand cupped one of her large breasts. It spilled out of his hands as he squeezed, making her lean closer. With a small popping noise, he released the now hardened nipple and looked up to meet her eyes.

"Now, 앉아," he commanded.

And she followed his order immediately. He slid into her so easily. Her arousal made it so simple. She let out a small squeak at the shock of how much he filled her. The feeling was all consuming.

"That's it," he praised. "You take my cock so well, Kat. I can feel you squeezing me."

Her whole body ignited under his admiration, and she sat up only to sit back down, but he met her with his own thrust, causing a much louder moan to escape her lips.

"씨발. Your moans make me fucking crazy ,애기." He grabbed her hips, making her grind against him. The way he rubbed her clit had her grabbing his shoulder to brace herself.

"지훈 that——" She couldn't focus on forming sentences as she bounced again, the bed making a slight squeaking noise that stole her focus on her pleasure and made herworry about her weight.

"Don't you dare stop riding my cock," he groaned. "I need to feel you cum on me."

"But the bed——"

He took her nipple into his mouth again, biting down as his hand reached around to give her a light, but still stinging, slap on her ass. Making her moan and grind on him again. He released her one nipple to take the other in his mouth, swirling his tongue, mimicking the soothing his hand was doing on her butt cheek. His hand went to her neck, where he slid two fingers up under her necklace and used it to pull her closer and have her eyes meet his.

"Focus on your pleasure. Don't worry about anything else." He brought her lips down to meet his and jutted his hips up. She moaned into his mouth, his tongue pushing inside hers. He was making her keep the focus. She grinded, and that's when she felt him hit the spot. The spot only her vibrator had ever found while she imagined it was 지훈. And she really *had* him. Under her. Inside her.

Holy shit! I am riding 지훈 of CLAR1T!

"Yes you are," 지훈 grunted in her ear. "You're doing such a good job."

Had she said that out loud? How could he have known what she was thinking?

"You're face gives everything away Kat. I told you that." He bit her earlobe as he pumped into her again, and she met his thrust, making her come back into the now of what they were doing. Her pace increased, the bed squeaking louder. And he met her pace, hitting the right spot repeatedly. She knew what was about to happen, and he must've sensed it as well.

"You are so fucking beautiful. I bet you're going to look even more stunning when you cum on my cock." He grabbed her chin, bringing her mouth back onto his. She closed her eyes as a heat built in her that was desperate for release. He grabbed her chin more forcefully.

"Look in my eyes when you come. I want to see just how much pleasure you get from finding the right spot using my cock." He smirked and licked her bottom lip as she continued her ride.

She followed his instruction as his hips met hers with strong pumps hitting that spot that made her legs shake. She had never been so close to climax with a man inside her. None had even come close to giving her the pleasure she desired.

But he was. 지훈 was about to shatter her into a million delicious pieces. Her pace sped up, and he again followed her lead, matching with his thrusts. Her moans were getting louder by the second.

"지훈!" she cried out, her eyes meeting his as her body came undone. He bit his lip as he grinned and continued to pump into her to let her ride out her high. Tiny but strong shocks of electricity shot through her. Her body shivered as she took in his eyes raking over her body and a proud smile at a job well done. And he had everything to be cocky about. As she continued to ride her high, his hand cupped her cheek but quickly began brushing strands of hair off her face.

"아름다워," he praised her as her orgasm finally faded, before he brought his lips to hers once again. "Let's see how many more we can get out of you."

KOREAN VOCABULARY:
앉아 – anja - sit

CHAPTER EIGHT

B efore Kat could say anything, they both turned their heads at the sound of a loud vibrating tone coming from the desk in the back of the room. She peered back at him, and his faced shared a perplexity most likely matching her own that, simultaneously with hers, turned to realization. Her phone must've turned on.

"핸드폰," he said between his heavy breaths.

"핸드폰," she repeated between her own.

"If she can get us out, and we leave here..." He grabbed her hand off his shoulder and kissed her fingers. "Please tell me we aren't done?"

She let out a small laugh, which brought his eyes to hers immediately. "We're not done. I still need to make you cum."

She kissed him quickly before lifting and feeling him slide out of her. Her legs were shaky and she grabbed onto the racks of set pieces as she took steady steps toward her phone, feeling her own pleasure dripping down her inner thighs. She was surprised to see no worried missed calls or texts from Dafne. Maybe her phone hadn't caught up yet. She wasted no time swiping it open to call Daf.

After only one ring she could hear a bunch of loud sounds followed by her best friend's voice. "Your night isn't over already, is it?"

"Daf, I'm locked in the theater and—"

"Yeah, I know," Dafne shouted over the deafening music wherever she was.

"What do you mean you know?" Kat's eyes met 지훈's as he started pulling up his pants to make his way over to her.

"Your little bias boy's friend and I made sure of it. He'll be by in the morning to come and get you guys out with a nice change of clothes for the both of you." Kat could hear several familiar laughs behind Dafne's voice.

"You're with CLARIT right now?!" Kat shouted as she saw 지훈's mouth drop in shock.

"Minus your man. Nice guys. I get why you like them so much." Kat could hear Daf's amusement through the phone. It was followed by several glasses clinking and a cheer of "짠!"

"See you tomorrow, bestie!" Daf shouted before there was silence on the line.

"Hello? Hell—" Kat pulled the phone from her ear to see the call had ended. "She hung up on me!"

"What did you mean she's with my groupmates?" 지훈 asked.

"은호 and Dafne *planned* this!" She began pacing back and forth in front of the desk. "And now they're with your entire group and from what I could hear they were drinking together."

While she was pacing, she wondered why he wasn't saying anything, and when she caught sight of him and his bare chest, she noticed his abs flexing. When she saw his face, she caught him laughing.

"You seriously laughing about us being locked in here right now? That our friends did this to us?" She walked over to him.

"네," he responded with a smile.

"네?" she repeated in shock.

"네. 정말 행복해." He pushed his hands into his sweatpants pockets. "I wanted to spend as much time as I could with you. And they gave me the whole night."

지훈 shook his head, his shoulders bobbing up and down as he laughed. His hand reached for hers. "Our friends seem to want us to spend this time together as well."

He pulled her closer. "I enjoy watching you pace totally naked, but being able to hold you totally naked is even more enjoyable."

She had completely forgotten the fact that she was naked, and still in the heels that she had been dying to get out of only a few hours ago.

"If we're here all night, why don't we make it count?" His fingers traced up the side of her body, causing her to shiver and press into his chest. He brought his lips to hers, warming her entire body. She wanted to memorize every ridge on his lips. Not only his lips, but every single bit of his body.

"You're right. We shouldn't waste another minute." She spoke against his lips as she poked at his tattoo, making them both smile. Her lips didn't stay on his for long. They trailed to that jawline she'd swooned over in images online, down his long neck.

"Please. 만져봐," he begged, and she felt his Adams apple bob against her lips.

Kat brought her hands to his chest, where she felt a large breath leave his body as she roamed the curves of his pecks. She caught his nipples hardening, and as she hid a devious smirk, she bent down and let her tongue flick the one hardened peak.

He growled, grabbing her hair and tugging, her eyes meeting his. But what she noticed more was how she enjoyed the sting of his grip on her hair just like she had enjoyed him giving her a small spank.

"You're playing a dangerous game there, 애기." He spoke with a breathless voice.

She knew exactly what she wanted to do, and she wasn't going to waste what little time they had together. With his hand still in her hair she began lowering herself, feeling and hearing her knees crack, but she kept her eyes on his. She watched as his went wide with surprise as she got to her knees, and her hands grabbed his waistband.

"Kat—" He exhaled her named as he gave another tug on her hair.

"I want to know what you like too," she whispered, tugging his sweats down to reveal the rock-hard cock she had come all over only a few minutes ago. "Show me?"

She leaned forward, kissing the tip of his cock, when she heard a groan and she watched as his head fell back. Hearing his enjoyment in her actions had her wet and aching for him again. She kissed down his cock to the base and licked back up. Getting a small taste of herself from earlier mixed with the delicious taste of him.

She took the head in her mouth, and his hand in her hair gripped tighter as his free hand leaned forward against the desk to brace himself.

"Kat," he moaned her name as her tongue swiped at the slit of his cock, making all other words seem to catch in his throat. The hand he had gripping onto her hair was pulling and she glanced up to see his eyes focused on her. She rubbed her thighs together to ease the ache, but she knew it wasn't going to be enough. She watched his mouth open and close a few times as he tried to form words. But all that did was give her an ego boost, and with no words spoken she pushed herself to take his whole cock in her mouth. It hit the back of her throat ,which made her gag.

When she heard no complaints, she did the move again, and then bobbed her head, taking in smaller amounts of his cock in her mouth. Her tongue swirled around the head before again taking him in to the hilt. His hand in her hair tugged every so often, but it was not to get her to stop. She even felt him push her to take more of his cock, which she happily obliged.

She loved how much he was enjoying it, and she wanted to enjoy it too. She spread her legs and slid a finger into her folds and circled her clit. Moaning with an overwhelm of pleasure vibrated his cock in her mouth.

"씨발. Are you playing with yourself, 애기?" He finally got a full sentence out.

She nodded with his cock still in her mouth.

"You like my cock down your throat that much you can't even

wait for it to be in that delicious pussy?" He definitely had caught his breath, and his deep, lustful voice had her circling her clit faster as she took him to the back of her throat again.

Her eyes watered as she continued to take his cock into her mouth and keep eye contact while she played with herself.

He started to press his hips to meet her mouth, and it began a faster pace, her gagging mixed with her own moans and his, building both their orgasms.

"Are you gonna swallow it all like a good girl?" he asked as his hips continued to push his cock into her mouth. She quickly nodded and started to play with herself faster.

That's when he took a few more quick but hard thrusts into her mouth, and she felt warm liquid coat her throat, choking her slightly, as a euphoric high spread throughout her own body.

She pulled her mouth away and felt a mix of saliva and his cum on the corners of her lips. As she wiped it away, his hand came to her cheek and wiped away the tears that had fallen.

"God you're beautiful," he whispered.

Her heart melted from the praise. 지훈 had called her beautiful. An idol she had thought she could only see through a computer screen or from the nosebleeds at a concert, having read countless fan fictions where the "Your Name" gets the idol they always wanted, had just looked at her and called her beautiful.

"This is a new type of fan service," she joked, which caused them both to let out a small chuckle.

"Let's get you cleaned up and go explore this place a bit, what do you say?" he asked, putting out his hand for her to take and help her get to her feet.

"As long as I can take these shoes off, absolutely." She hobbled to the bed, where she kicked off the heels, and the instant relief she felt caused her to let out a moan.

"Kicking off shoes can cause that kind of moan but I can't?" he laughed as he pulled up his sweats and walked over to her.

"시끄러워,"she laughed as she rubbed her feet to relieve some of the swelling.

"여기." He grabbed his hoodie off the bed. "I know you don't want to put that dress back on."

"고마워." She happily took the hoodie. When she put her arms into the holes, the sweatshirt scrunched up against her chest and she was hit with his sexy scent. She tried very hard not to sniff it like a creeper as she tossed it over her head.

"Looks good on you." He tugged one of the strings on the hood.

"Luckily you love to wear oversized clothing, otherwise this would've been kind of embarrassing for me." She smiled, pushing her hands into the front pocket. He let out a huff with a pouted bottom lip.

"Luckily, I think you look stunning in anything, preferably nothing. In fact, I wish it didn't fit so I could have you completely bare and I could enjoy every inch of your beauty." He crossed his arms in front of his bare chest as he gave a once-over.

"Come on, let's explore." He changed the subject as he put out his hand for her to take, and what concerned her was how much she enjoyed the simple act of him holding her hand. That whole "he's an idol she could 'like' from a far" had become a man she learned personal things about, had sex with, and just gave a blow job to. And he was someone who, in a few short hours, would become that unobtainable idol once again.

She wasn't sure her heart could handle what she agreed to earlier in the evening.

KOREAN VOCABULARY:

핸드폰 – haendeupon – cellphone
짠 – jjan – cheers
정말 행복해 – jeongmal haengboghae – I'm really happy
만져봐 – manjyeobwa – touch me
시끄러워 – sikkeuleowo – literal translation is "noisy," but it's used as the phrase "be quiet" or "shut up"
여기 – yeogi – here
고마워 – gomawo – thank you (informal)

CHAPTER NINE

"You ready?" 지훈 asked in the darkened hallway he was pulling her down. He had listened to Kat open up about the insecurities she struggled with. He could tell it had been hard for her to be so open, and so he wanted to share some of his own demons. Besides being fair, being with her was the most at ease he had felt in years.

"뭐가?" she asked just as he pulled open a black curtain to reveal he had led them to the stage.

"One day I want to perform on this stage," he admitted as he walked them to the middle of the empty stage.

"I know one day you will. And even bigger stages too." She smiled as she squeezed his hand. He loved holding her, any piece of her he could. When he let go, that ease he felt dissipated, and so he would keep her near him the rest of the night.

He gave her a little twirl on the stage and pulled her back against his chest, holding her against him as they gently swayed.

"I dreamed of performing overseas ever since I became a trainee." He sighed. "But after a few months of being a trainee, that dream had started to shatter as the company didn't think I was going to make it into any of the groups they were planning. My vocals aren't the best, all I had was my dancing. So they thought I should become a choreographer for the groups they did plan to debut."

"What!" She turned her body around in his arms, her sweater paws in his hoodie pressed against his bare chest.

"I accepted it. At least I would have a job doing something I love. Maybe my name wouldn't be in lights across the world, but I could see my name in credits. And so I danced." He continued to sway them, his hands lifting up his hoodie behind her to fiddle with her butt cheeks. "I got an opportunity to perform in another group's music video, and the one member liked my style so much that he asked me to choreograph his upcoming solo release."

He reached to grab her hand off his chest and gave her another twirl, bringing her warmth back into his embrace as he continued to open up.

"Which made me believe the company was right, I wasn't meant to be in the spotlight." Her eyes weren't leaving his. Her lips pouted with concern, but then she opened her mouth and her eyes went wide.

"Oh wait! I remember that! Twitter blew up about the sexy background dancer in the 하룻밤만 video." She laughed.

"My agency took notice of that and changed their mind about letting me debut in a group. I was tossed into CLARIT only a few months before they were set to debut." He tugged her even closer to him if that was possible.

"I'm glad they did." She leaned up and pecked him gently on the lips. "You deserve all that you've accomplished and will accomplish."

He was touched by her kindness. Kat might've been a fan, but he could feel her sincerity.

"When I injured myself right after our debut…" He didn't think he would choke up, but the fear he had when it happened resurfaced the second he brought it up. Fracturing his wrist was one of the most terrifying moments in his life, not because of the pain, but because of what it could have meant for his career, his dreams. He raised his arm and showed the small scar where he had a plate and pin placed to fix the fracture.

"You were scared they were going to kick you out of the group?" Kat asked, releasing one of her sweater paws to bring her warm hand to his cheek.

"I hadn't been with the boys all that long at that point, so it wouldn't have been a big deal for them to drop me," he explained. "I was ready for it. I wasn't really, but I wouldn't have been surprised."

"But you weren't dropped. The boys stood by you, correct?"

He could tell she was trying to cheer him up. Bring him out of the dark days of the past like he had been trying to do for her.

"They did. They even spoke to our management, saying they wouldn't continue as a group if I wasn't part of CLARIT. It took me by surprise." He leaned into her warm touch. He had never opened up about his fear of being booted from CLARIT. "They were with me the entire time, helping me do my stretches, even changing choreo so I could still perform with them and not fuck up my wrist.It doesn't feel real sometimes. I felt like I didn't deserve everything they did for me." Tears fell from his eyes, which Kat quickly wiped away.

"Would you have done the same for one of them if it had been the other way around?" she asked.

"당연하죠." As if that was even a question. He would do anything for the boys. They had become his family.

"Then why do *you* think you deserve less?" she argued. It was a valid point that left him speechless. "Everyone doubts their self-worth. I'm also guilty of it. I know it's something I'm still working on every day. But you should know, as your fan and friend for the evening, how insanely talented you are."

She pulled away from him and took a seat on the stage, patting the spot next to her, so he sat down.

"Your dancing was what first caught my attention when CLARIT debuted. I have been into K-pop for many years and have stanned many groups, but I'm not kidding when I say, when I saw you come out in the costume for 이리 와 I quickly began to google names to find out who you were." She laughed.

"A couple million people would agree with me," she continued, "including your own groupmates, that CLAR1T wouldn't be what they are without you and your talent." She grabbed his hand again and brought it to her lips. Her warmth spread through him like a fire. But that's when he felt a wet drip on the back of his hand. When she looked back up at him, he saw tears falling down her cheeks.

"고마워," he choked out as tears welled in his own eyes, and before he knew it, more poured out and they both reached out to wipe the tears off one another's cheeks.

"Hey, I'm supposed to be the one comforting you!" she joked, which made him smile.

"This time I'm not trying to comfort you." He smiled as he watched her eyebrows scrunch together and her lips turn down into a frown. "I'm doing this so I can commit your warmth and kindness to memory any time I need cheering up."

She laughed. "That's so cheesy."

"Try to cover up that you enjoy it." He pinched her cheek, turning the tears from sad to happy. And she giggled.

"You have an addicting laugh," he complimented as he caught his breath.

She responded, "And this is your real laugh that not many people have heard before."

His eyes widened and he stuttered to try to find an answer, but he couldn't. She had figured out something he wasn't expecting. He leaned forward and kissed her softly.

"맞아," he admitted before kissing her again. Her tongue slipped into his mouth, making him growl. His lips left hers to trail down her neck, and he sucked gently.

"Mark me," she whispered, and it sent heat right down to his cock. "You can mark me anywhere you want. It'll be a reminder, at least for a little while, that this night actually happened."

He didn't hesitate to nip the area he had just been sweetly

sucking on. She moved her head to the side to give him more access to her deliciously soft and sweet neck. But he pulled away.

"잠시만." His eyes wandered around as he tried to determine how he could also have something to remember her by. And suddenly it felt like all those cartoons where the light bulb turned on above his head. He grinned at her.

"I want you to mark me as well."

"뭐라고? You can't have any kind of— Fans will... What?" She stumbled trying to piece together what he was asking.

"You can't make them obvious. No neck, but I tend to keep the rest of my body covered, especially since I got the tattoo, so anywhere else is fair game." He waved his hands along his torso. He leaned all the way back, his back hitting the cold floor of the stage. He was like a kid in a candy shop, excitement coursing through his body, wondering where she would choose.

"Are you sure?" she nervously asked, but her eyes were trained on his torso. She must've had a place in mind.

"Kathleen." He used her full name, knowing it would bring all her attention to him. "For as long as this mark is on my body, I. Am. Yours."

He watched as her lips parted, her eyes filled with more than lust.

"지훈," she said softly as she leaned over to kiss him. The kiss shared more than just a physical attraction, he could tell she was trying to convey something deeper.

"애기, please," he begged her again. He wasn't ashamed to beg. He wanted to show her how desperate she made him to have her affection. And it must've done the trick because she threw her one leg over him to straddle his torso, her hands on his chest, and her lips began their descent down his body. His hands went to her bare thighs. Thighs he was having so many visions of crushing his head as he tasted that gorgeous cunt of hers.

He gripped them even harder as she shimmied down, her lips taking in one of his nipples and flicking it, before moving to the other to make another deliciously painful hard peak.

"Fuck, 애기," he moaned.

73

She sat up and he watched as her eyes scanned over his body and her hands explored it. She paused on the side of his torso. The side where his tattoo was as she moved farther down his body, his hands no longer able to grab her thighs, leaving him feeling empty. She bent down again, kissing his abs, licking down the maze of each muscle before landing right near the tattoo.

Her eyes looked up to meet his, and if his cock wasn't already begging to get out of his pants again, it was about to rip itself out to be inside her again. And as he kept thinking about the positions he wanted her in, he felt her bite down on his side, before gently swirling her tongue and sucking the spot she had marked.

"That's it, 애기." He loved watching the blush cover her body when he gave her any sort of encouragement. And she moved down to his pelvis to make another mark on him.

"Get up here," he commanded and felt her shiver and her thighs clench against him. She enjoyed him telling her what to do as much as she enjoyed having him beg for her to do it. She slowly moved back up his body, her lips tripping up his chest before meeting his hungrily, as his hands played around her waist, pushing the hoodie up, revealing the sweet skin beneath it.

"I meant all the way up here." He reached his hand between them and slid a finger between her wet folds. She was dripping for him again.

"지훈, no. I would suffocate you." She tried to pull away, lift her leg to no longer straddle him, but he held her legs and even started to pull her upward. He wasn't going to let her go.

"Sounds like a great time to me." He winked. If she wasn't going to move up to him, he would happily shimmy down to her.

"I don't know." She bit her lip, and he could see her contemplating.

"I do. I want to eat you out, while you ride my face. As hard as you want. Remember tonight is all for your pleasure, 애기." He slid down while simultaneously pulling her up. Getting her closer, he could smell her arousal, and his body hummed to get a taste. But he could tell she was still extremely nervous.

"We can start slow. You straddle my face, I'll do the rest. If you still feel uncomfortable after I start, we can switch it up. But I've tasted you on your fingers and I'm dying to taste you directly."

There was the blush he enjoyed seeing so much. He loved that what he said could have such an effect.

Instead of giving him a response, he felt her move up his body, and he readied himself to be faced with the feast he'd been craving since laying his eyes on her. He trailed kisses up each of her inner thighs. He felt them shake harder with every kiss closer to her center.

His tongue took its first pass through her slit, and it was sweeter than he could've ever imagined. She tasted like honey. His nose brushed her clit and she dropped closer to him. 완벽해. His hands traced up and down her thighs as his tongue continued to swipe her core before gently sucking her clit and then plunging his tongue into her cunt.

"Fuck," she moaned, which encouraged him to continue.

He pulled away from the deliciousness of her to speak. "If you just started riding my face, it would feel even better. 약속해."

"무서워." She brought her hands to her cheeks. "I've never done something like this. I've read it countless times. But what if I really hurt you?"

He brought his hands to her ass and tapped. "If I can't handle something, I'll do this. How about that?"

She didn't say anything, turning her head over her shoulder to see his hand on her ass. He worried he had ruined the mood and just as he was about to tell her it was okay and they didn't need to continue, he heard it.

"Okay," she agreed.

His heart sang. His breaths became shallow in anticipation.

"Good, 애기. Now…" He paused, his tongue giving her cunt a swipe before finishing, "앉아."

And like the good girl she was, she dropped down, and he became a man who was being fed after starving for months. In all honesty he had been starving for close to two years. Dance training, recording, preparing for debut took up ninety percent of his time.

Sex had rarely crossed his mind, and if it did, his hand usually did the trick.

When he saw Kat as a seat filler—her smile, her eyes, the way she lit up when someone complimented her—she had him on the edge of his seat the entire event, and he knew his hand wouldn't cut it that night. His tongue hit her clit, and she ground into him, his tongue slipping inside her.

She liked that motion because he felt her repeat it. His tongue flicked her clit and she ground into him, making his tongue slip inside her again.

"씨발," he mumbled against her, and she lifted herself off him a bit. It gave him the access to get his hand between her legs so he could slip his fingers inside her as well.

He grabbed her thigh with his free hand to pull her back down in place. He wasn't going to let her go until she came on his face.

"You taste like heaven, 애기." He pressed her back down onto his face and he sucked, swirled, and swiped his tongue all over her as he let her ride his fingers to help him find the right spots.

"지훈, I—" She wasn't able to string a full sentence together, and he knew what that meant.

"You wanna cum?" he asked, and he couldn't hear a response. "Use your words, Kathleen," he said before nipping on her clit, making her sit hard on his face. Breathing was becoming a problem and he was loving every second of it.

"네!" she screamed as her body shuddered, her orgasm ripping through her, squeezing his fingers and dripping all over his face. He continued sucking and licking, not wanting to waste a drop. Committing her delicious honey flavor to memory.

She hadn't moved for a few seconds, and before he started to worry that he would have to tap her ass, she pulled herself up, moving down his torso to look down at him with wide eyes, rosy cheeks, and her mouth open as she was still catching her breath.

"I wanna do that again." He smiled as he licked her flavor on his lips and used his thumb to catch the rest.

"Me too." She grinned back, and his heart did a small flip. Her glow was even more radiant after she admired her cum all over his face. And then she said something that made his heart explode.

"I want you inside me again."

KOREAN VOCABULARY:

하룻밤만 – halusbamman – only one night

당연하죠 – dang-yeonhajyo – of course

이리 와 – ili wa – come on

맞아 – maja – correct

잠시만 – jamsiman – hold on (informal)

뭐라고? – mwolago? – what?

완벽해 – wanbyeoghae – perfect

약속해 – yagsoghae – I promise

무서워 – museowo – I'm scared

CHAPTER TEN

Kat had to suppress the laugh as she stared below her and saw the shock on 지훈's face. But she really had to contain herself when she followed up with, "And I want you to show me how you like it."

"Kat I—" He was fumbling.

"Oh, I mean if you're not—" She lifted her leg and climbed off him.

"Kat don't let your mind go where it's about to go." He sat up quickly, reaching for her hands. He took a deep breath and grabbed her chin to make sure her eyes were on him. "I've been holding back this entire night. If you're giving me the go ahead, I won't be able to suppress myself anymore."

"Why were you holding back to begin with?" She couldn't keep her eyes off his lips. Lips she had traced on the photocards she collected. Lips that had been on hers, on her body, and just made her cum. They were swollen lips that she wanted to kiss again, that she wanted all over her body.

"You never had someone learn what you like, and I wasn't about to be another one of those assholes." He grabbed her hand with a nice squeeze in comfort. She wasn't sure if it was for her or himself.

"You deserve to feel amazing, and fuck did it feel good to have you cum on my cock and in my mouth." His finger that held her chin brought her face closer to his. "I haven't had sex in two years," he admitted.

"뭐?!" she exclaimed louder than she meant to.

"I haven't had the time. Or the interest, if I'm being honest." He brought his nose to hers, slowly tracing it. "If you tell me to show you what I like, I won't be able to control myself. Because the things I want to do to you—"

"What do you want to do to me?" She let her tongue slip out and licked his top lip. His eyes closed and his jaw clenched several times.

"I want to take you from behind. I want to spank that delicious ass until it's bright red. I want to pull your hair back so I can get my other hand around your neck and edge you so many times it becomes torture until we come together." He played her game and his tongue licked her top lip before taking it into his mouth and biting it.

Holy fucking shit. Kat wasn't expecting a confession like that. She also wasn't expecting how exciting all of that sounded.

"그럼," she started, backing her face away from his and positiong herself on all fours, "what're you waiting for?"

He wasted no time pulling off his sweatpants, and she watched his cock spring out as he motioned for her to lift her knees. Sliding his sweatpants under her legs, he created makeshift padding for her knees.

"Take off the sweatshirt," he commanded and she followed his instruction quickly. "That's my 애기."

"My?" she raised a mocking brow, "No more 우리, I've noticed."

"No. You're mine. All mine." His hand traced down her spine and grabbed her ass before she heard a loud smack and felt a sting. She let out a shocked squeak, but she found she enjoyed the stinging sensation. Before she could tell him she was okay, another smack and stinging sensation on her other cheek.

He spread her legs and slid into her, filling her completely. She choked back her shock at how wet she already was that he slid in so easily. He gave her ass another smack as he pulled back and entered her again. She moved back to meet his thrust.

"You like a little pain with your pleasure, huh, 애기?" His voice was rough. While she couldn't see him, she sensed that he had his teeth gritted as he pounded into her again. Every thrust brought a growing high. She moved to meet his thrusts and he would spank her even harder.

And just like he said, he wrapped his one hand in her hair pulling her head back and his other hand went to her neck, his chest against her back.

"If you can't handle it tap the floor, 알았지?" he whispered in her ear.

"네," she moaned.

"That's my good girl." His hand on her throat gently pressed, and she closed her eyes to take in the thrill of the lack of air, his hand tugging in her hair, and his cock pushing deep inside her. It was sensation overload, and she could feel pleasure building in her body.

"I feel you squeezing me. You want to cum don't you?" he asked, releasing her throat to let her speak.

"네." She nodded, his hand tugging her hair.

"Not yet." He rotated his hips, hitting a whole new angle that had her moaning through the pressure on her throat. "씨발. You take my cock so fucking good."

He was relentless, and she could feel the orgasm building again, but he slowed, cutting off the high once more. Her frustration made her press back into him, desperate to get that feeling back. His hand tugged her hair harder, making her moan louder, but then he pressed on her throat, cutting off her moan.

"I'm going to count us down, Kat. You cum when I say you can." His voice was gruff, like the wind had been knocked out of him.

"셋," he began, his hand in her hair pulling tighter.

"둘," his hand on her throat pressed harder.

"하나." He let go of her throat and brought his fingers to her

81

clit. His pace was relentless, and all she could see was red. The explosion of her orgasm was so powerful as she maintained her pace as he reached his own high.

"Kat," she heard him moan from behind her as her orgasm slowly wore off. "Kat," he repeated.

"네?" she breathlessly whispered.

"괜찮아?" His hand traced up and down her spine softly. A total juxtaposition to what he had been doing only a minute or two before.

"네." She nodded as her knees finally gave out, and she rolled over and onto the cool floor of the stage.

He laughed. "Is that all you know how to say now?"

"You fucked me stupid," she laughed back.

She didn't hear a response, and when she leaned her head up, she saw there was no one on the stage with her.

"지훈?" She sat up, searching for any signs of him. Panic began to set in as a feeling of abandonment started to creep its way through her body. She reached for his hoodie to cover herself, and as she was putting it over her head, she heard footsteps.

When her head popped out of the opening, she saw his totally naked frame walking toward her. When the calm started to knock out the negativity, she took in the sight of 지훈 completely bare. His chest, his abs, the tattoo, the V of his pelvis bringing full attention to his cock. A cock she'd had in her mouth, and inside her.

"I grabbed a clean towel to help clean up." He waved the towel in his hand.

"Oh, I thought you—" She cut herself off. She knew he wouldn't like what she was about to say, and she knew she shouldn't have thought he would've done such a thing.

"Fuck, Kat." His pace picked up to kneel in front of her. "미안. I should've said something before just walking off. I didn't think—"

"It's not your fault." She shook her head.

"Have men really just up and left with no word?" he asked.

Her throat closed up and all she could do was nod.

"I will *never* leave you like that. Understand me?" He cupped her cheek and brought his lips to hers. It was him confirming his state-ment to her, and it soothed her. But she had to be realistic.

"But you will, come tomorrow morning." She was nervous about how he would take the statement. He stared at her. His lips dipped down to a frown before shaking his head, dropping it as he brought the towel between her legs and gently cleaned the mess they had made.

She flinched at the cool sensation, but once it warmed on her skin it was very soothing. After a minute, he pulled away and grabbed his sweats off the floor, standing.

"We should get some rest." He put out his hand for her to take.

"Rest?" she asked.

"If you think because I'm letting us get some sleep, it means we're done, you're very wrong." His smile was wide, but the happi-ness didn't meet his eyes.

She didn't want to open that door just yet, and so she took his hand and they slowly walked back to the prop room where the bed was. He dropped her hand once inside and searched the shelves, finally pulling out a blanket.

"우리 자자." He climbed onto the bed and gently patted the space beside him.

She sat beside his prostrate frame and stared down at him. "고마워."

"응?" He propped his head up on his hand.

"For tonight, thank you. I will never forget it." She smiled, but her heart was already hurting. She knew what was going to happen. She'd known what she was getting herself into, and yet her heart had decided it wasn't going to accept it. She was going to get hurt, but this time she did it knowingly; she hoped that would make the healing process quicker.

"You're in your head, Kat." He reached up to brush her hair away from her face and behind her ear. "뭘 그렇게 생각해?."

She loved how well he could read her and bring her back into the now. With a soft smile she lay down and turned to face him.

"Let's rest a bit." He wrapped an arm around her waist, his hand landing on the small of her back, and his fingers stroked up and down her spine. "I'm going to need you well rested when I tie you to this bed and make you cum on my cock several more times."

"You're ridiculous," she laughed, pushing his chest.

"You do it to me, 애기." He smiled and leaned over to kiss her. "좋은 꿈 꿔."

KOREAN VOCABULARY:

그럼 – geuleom – well then

알았지? – al-assji? – understand?

셋 – set – three

둘 – dul – two

하나 – hana – one

우리 자자 – uli jaja – let's sleep

응? – eung? – another kind of catch all. In this instance, it's being used to imply "for what?"

뭘 그렇게 생각해? – mwol geuleohge saeng-gaghae? – what are you thinking so hard about?

좋은 꿈 꿔 – joh-eun kkum kkwo – sweet dreams

CHAPTER ELEVEN

He wasn't kidding when he told Kat that he would be tying her to the bed and making her cum many times. She woke up to him kissing her neck, down her breasts, and when she tried to grab his head she realized her hands couldn't move. There had been a second of panic until she realized he had used the drawstring of his sweatpants to tie her to the metal of the headboard. When she caught his stare she was met with a smirk as he kissed down her belly and landed between her legs.

After he had made her cum twice with his tongue, then put one of her legs on his shoulder and one around his hip and pounded into her relentlessly, causing another orgasm to rip through her along with him reaching his climax simultaneously.

He pulled out of her, laying to her side and untied her, kissing her reddening wrists before he got up to find the towel to help clean her up. They spent a few minutes catching their breath when she heard her phone vibrating over and over and over again. She moved to stand and felt her whole body aching.

As she made her way to the phone, she knew what the call was. Their time was up.

She saw Dafne's name pop up, as expected.

"Hey, Daf." Kat's greeting was cold. It wasn't her being mad at the call, but being sad that the night had come to an end.

"은호 should be there in ten minutes. He'll meet you at the seats you first sat in," she said nonchalantly, but it was followed by a groan.

"You okay?" Kat asked.

"Have you heard of 소주? Those boys can pound it back like water. I'm hungover as shit. But be at those seats in ten minutes, okay?" Dafne grumbled.

"Okay, we will be there." She didn't want to talk to Dafne any more in that moment. She had to face that her time with 지훈was up. Her one night with her ultimate bias had come to an end.

"만두," 지훈 said.

"What?" She turned to him, wondering why he had randomly mentioned dumplings.

"At the beginning of the night you asked what my secret word was with my groupmates. It's 만두." He stood up from the bed and walked toward her.

"That's weirdly very fitting." She laughed.

"If you needed one, what do you think yours would be?" he asked.

"Easy. Waffles." She smiled, picturing exactly what she was going to eat the second she got out of that theater to wallow in the sadness of never again seeing the only man who not only made her cum more times than she could count, but the man who made her feel her sexiest and most beautiful. Their connection was more than physical. He was someone she confided in, and he trusted her with some of his secrets as well.

"We need to meet 은호 where we first met." She picked at her nails before her hands were covered by his and he brought them to his lips. "Guess I gotta put my dress back on. Don't think your groupmate wants to see my bare ass."

"*I* don't want him to see that gorgeous bare ass. 내꺼야." He reached around and grabbed a handful, pulling her to him, and covered her lips with his.

She pushed him off, though. For two reasons. One, they needed to get down to the seats. Two, she needed to keep distance between them for those last few moments they would be together. If not, she wouldn't be able to walk away once they were out of the theater.

She covered up her sadness with an attempt at lightheartedness. "If you keep that up, we won't meet up with 은호."

"That's fine by me. I'd rather spend the day in this prop room with you, than in a green room with five other men." He started pecking kisses all over her face.

"Holy shit, it's your first show of the tour tonight! How could I have forgotten that?" Her fangirl was coming out. His smile grew wide before kissing her again.

"I almost forgot I was your ultimate bias." He laughed. She rolled her eyes, feeling the blush creep up, and she dropped her head to his chest. "Am I still?"

Her head shot up to see if he was asking seriously. And she could see hope in his eyes, but his jaw clenched and unclenched with nerves.

"My only bias, 지훈아." She lifted onto her tiptoes to gently kiss his lips. Savoring them one last time. "Now let's get down to the seats."

은호 ARRIVED SEVERAL MINUTES LATER. HE HAD SOMEHOW convinced the building's management that he lost his cellphone the night before. With the alarm being shut off, they could exit out a side door without anyone noticing.

He handed 지훈 a bag full of clothing. 지훈 unpacked it to see he had packed a bunch of tour merch for Kat to wear. She left the two men to go to change in the bathroom. The bathroom where everything started. Reality hit her immediately—the second they walked out the doors of the theater, it was over. A memory.

She let her tears fall for a minute before pulling herself together enough to change and get back out to say her final goodbye. She found the two idols standing together.

"We found a door that you and I can take while 은호 goes back

out the front," 지훈 explained. She went to hand him back the hoodie he had let her borrow for the night. "What're you doing?"

"Giving you your stuff back," she said, stating the obvious.

"It isn't mine anymore." He pushed it back toward her and leaned down to whisper in her ear, "Wear it anytime you miss me. Or if you need something to help you get off."

She let out a shaky breath, trying to keep it together for her last few moments with him.

"You two done?" 은호 cut into the conversation. "I don't know how much longer I have before the guard comes to ask what's taking so long. We also need to get a move on to our venue before our management wonders where we are."

"내 형. We're ready." 지훈's eyes didn't leave hers as he spoke. His hand grabbed hers and gently pulled for her to follow. They made it to the side door, and she watched his shoulders rise and then drop as he loudly exhaled. Could he be feeling the same way as her?

He pushed the door open, and the chill of the LA morning air hit their faces along with the city smells.

"Do you have a way home?" he asked.

"I can call an Uber." She pulled out her phone. "You should probably go catch up with 은호."

He stood still, his hand keeping a hold on her.

"What if—" He stopped, taking another deep breath. "What if we don't say goodbye?"

"What?"

"What if we don't let this be the last time we see each other? What if we stay in touch? We have each other's phone numbers. We can text, call, video call."

"While I would love to, I don't think it would work." They needed to stick to the agreement. One night. That's it.

"왜?" He squeezed her hand hard. Maybe in order to keep her close for however much longer he could. But they both needed to face their reality: that they were from different worlds.

"We said it would be one night." She spoke as coldly as she could muster. "We wouldn't work past that."

"Kat, you can't possibly still only want one night." He took a step closer to her.

"What I want and what's the smart decision are two totally different things." She was doing her best to hold herself together, but if they stood there any longer, she wasn't sure she would be able to control her emotions.

"But—"

"Please don't make this harder than it already is, 지훈." She pulled her hand free from his and reached around to the back of her neck to find the clasp of her necklace. She released its clasp and dropped the chains into his hand. "I will always be your fan, 지훈, and I will support you from where I always have. Last night was something out of a fan fiction. I will never forget it. 고마워."

She couldn't let him try to argue with her, because in all honesty he probably would've convinced her to try what he was offering. Her heart simply couldn't handle trying to be friends with the idol she had admired from afar, the man she had opened up to and let herself be free with. It scared her that those were one and the same. She turned the corner out of the small alley and was in the midst of downtown LA.

As she walked away, her phone vibrated, and she nervously looked, thinking he would be texting her instead of chasing her down, but she saw it was Dafne calling.

"Yeah, Daf," Kat sighed.

"Whoa that's not the reaction I was expecting from you after spending the whole night with the man you have been obsessing over for the last year plus." Daf's voice, while filled with sarcasm, also held a tone of worry.

"Daf..." Kat couldn't get any more words out before the dam broke and she began sobbing, her heart shattering to thousands of pieces.

"Shit. Get home ASAP. I'll be ready with all the usual heart menders."

"Extra waffles please," Kat choked out.

"Of course."

When she hung up to order the ride home, she saw a text. The text she had thought she was receiving only a minute earlier.

지훈: **I know you wouldn't want me to chase you. I understand your concern about us and I'm not going to pressure you into something that will cause you pain. I felt something last night. Not just the physical side, but we shared secrets, and more and more I begged for you to tell me more. I want to be someone you can trust. Please give me that chance.**

He knew all the right things to say to make her reconsider walking away. Hell, she even turned toward the theater, thinking she could run back and see him again. But just as she took the first step, her car arrived.

And so she ghosted 지훈 one last time.

KOREAN VOCABULARY:

소주 – soju – soju

만두 – mandu – dumplings

내꺼야 – naekkeoya – it's mine

지훈아 – jihuna – Ji-Hun (informal) a more affectionate form of someone's name

왜? – wae? – why?

CHAPTER TWELVE

F *ive months later...*
"Kat, I need you to grab some of the fake peonies and roses, and those strings of pearls from the closet," Daf shouted from beside the table where they were setting up to shoot a new jewelry collection.

Almost everything about the company was on the down-low; no one in the studio knew the company's name. All the products were sent in unmarked boxes, and even the return address was a vague warehouse.

Everyone had begun taking guesses at who the products were designed by and what company they were for, but it had remained a total mystery. The necklace they were in the midst of styling was a pretty double-strand snake and chain link with a very dainty heart in the center. Kat really wanted to know the brand because it was so gorgeous, and she wanted to purchase it when it was released.

"On it!" Kat shouted as she jogged down the small hall to start digging through all the fake flower boxes in the prop room.

When she found the ones she had been looking for, she started digging to find a soft pastel pallet of peonies and roses that she thought Daf would like for their concept.

SAMANTHA ANN

She heard the door open behind her.

"I'm looking, Daf, I just don't know if I should do pastel purple or shades of pinks and red." She raised the different colors up above her head for Dafne to see.

There was no response, but she heard the door close. *Guess that was the answer she was looking for.*

"This room's a bit smaller than the last one, don't you think?" She froze in place at the voice. It was a voice she heard in her head constantly and expected to never hear again outside albums and interviews. The voice of the man she had fallen in love with but chose to ghost because "logic" told her a relationship would never work out.

"I'm hearing things again," she whispered to herself, shaking off the feeling that someone was still in the closet with her. But instead of ridding the sensation, it grew like the person had moved closer.

"Again?" he responded with a dark laugh that sounded like it held anguish. "If you're hearing things, so am I, 애기."

No fucking way. She slowly turned her head, and there he was. Dressed in an oversized flowy white button-up tucked into the front of khaki pants that were held up by a rich tan leather belt. His hair was styled up and back away from his face, flaunting his thick brows just above eyes that glittered with hope, and a smile on his beautiful lips that held optimism.

"What the hell are you doing here? How are you here? What is going on?" She shot up looking all around the room for some cameras because it had to be some prank for a show.

"You ghosted me yet again. For five months this time." He took a step closer to her as he latched his hands behind him. He pulled his bottom lip between his teeth, and his deliciously sharp jaw clenched a few times.

"So you decided to figure out where I work and show up to lock us in the prop closet five months later?" She clutched the fake flowers so hard, the fake thorns were about to break the skin of her palm.

"Not exactly." He laughed. She still was unable to process him

92

standing in front of her. "You're photographing some jewelry today, correct?"

She nodded.

"A necklace? 목걸이?" He raised an eyebrow.

"How did you—" She stopped herself.

"Dafne and 은호 have been keeping in touch," he started. "In fact they've become quite the duo. Don't think they've slept together, but I can tell 은호 likes her a lot."

He took another step toward her. She stayed silent as she waited for him to continue.

"CLAR1T wanted to create some commemorative merch for our first US tour. We've all designed something uniquely us from our experiences on this tour. 은호 mentioned your company to our management team, saying he thought you would be a great fit for our products." Another step forward, and she felt his warmth.

"And you chose a necklace?" Kat asked as she craned her neck to see his chiseled bone structure.

"마자. It was the moment I first got to touch you." He leaned forward, his shirt dropping to give her a view of his strong bare chest and then a shimmering gold chain.

"And Dafne knew?" She forced herself to pull her stare away from the similar necklace and his chest, to avoid the memories of their night that flooded back, making her hot as a blush crept up her cheeks.

"She did. And I asked her to make sure you had no clue. Leave you guessing as much as I have been these last few months," he whispered, his minty breath fanning across her face.

"You mean—"

"I knew you would be here. And I knew I had to get you alone and ask for one more shot at more time with you. And not just another night, but as many nights and days as we possibly can have. I want it all with you. After you left the theater, all I could think about was how I wanted more."

"More?" she asked, and the hope in his eyes emanated through him to her.

"I wanted to know everything about you. Every last thing about you. What you like, don't like. What makes you smile, cry, laugh." His hand grabbed hers and it lit her entire body like only he had been able to do.

"보고 싶어. I've thought about you every day since we parted ways. I texted you—"

"I know." She cut him off.

"And you never responded?" he asked, his jaw clenching another few of times.

"I wanted to, but…" She stalled, trying to figure out how to explain. "I read every text you sent. It's such a cliché, but it wasn't you, it was me. I feared how attached I would become if I were to respond. And I was frightened by what would happen when you would inevitably change your mind."

"Why? I wanted you attached. I was attached. I still am." He placed his other hand on her hip, pulling her gently, closing all space between their bodies. "My mind hasn't changed in five months, and we haven't even spoken. I want all of you. Everything."

"My past, my mind… I kept telling myself it wasn't real or it was—" She cut herself off, knowing he would stop her from finishing the sentence.

"I fell in love with you that night," he blurted out. "That sounds crazy. Love at first sight, love at first night, whatever you want to call it, but it's what happened." He leaned his head down and touched his forehead to hers.

Her breath had been taken away. She looked all over his face. He was in love with her. He was standing in front of her professing his love for her.

"I know you. I know what you assumed of me." His breath warmed her skin. "You anticipated that I was like the men in your past. But I'm not. I never was and never will be, Kat."

"I know that…now." She reached into her back pocket to pull out her phone and open up her texts. "I never blocked you like you thought." She cupped his cheek with her free hand. "I should've told you what was on my mind. I should've said what I was worried about instead of shutting you out. But I made the decision alone to just avoid you. And I regret it so much."

She let tears fall down her cheeks. "If I wasn't so stupid, I probably would've said I fell in love with you that night as well. And by the time I realized my stupidity, you had stopped messaging me and I knew—"

His lips crushed hers. If her eyes weren't open she wouldn't believe 지훈 had been the one kissing her. His tongue slid along her bottom lip, taking in some of her tears as well. She melted into him, wrapping her arms around his neck to press her body harder into his.

"Fuck, 애기," he moaned as he pulled his lips from hers. She sighed at hearing him use his pet name for her again. "I've missed you, everything about you."

"나도." She leaned up to meet his lips again. "I'm not going to run away again. 약속해. I'm here. I'm in this. If you want to—"

He cut her off again with a forceful kiss. "You think I would be trying to figure out how to fuck you right here before your boss realizes you're missing if I wasn't in this?"

She shuddered with pleasure as memories of their night together came flooding back.

"I was in this from the moment I walked in that theater. I never fucking left, 애기." He pushed her back against one of the shelving units, his hands roaming her body and getting a good squeeze of her breasts.

"We can enjoy each other once we finish the shoot," she said before she bit his lip, which was rewarded with a growl and his hard cock pressing against her stomach.

"I'm holding you to that." He kissed her again before releasing her all together. "But wait."

He moved his hand away, digging into his pocket and pulling something out. "This was the first prototype."

He opened his hand, and a double-strand gold necklace dropped down, held between two of his fingers. It was almost identical to the one she wore the night they met, but there was a small lock on the thinner chain. Her lungs lost all oxygen, her skin tingled, and she had to lean against the shelf behind her to catch herself.

"I felt the lock was something only you deserved. Because that night being locked in that theater with you changed my life. The lock is for the one person who I trust with some of my darkest thoughts and desires. It's locked and the key is thrown away because you're the only one I want. The only one I love." He moved closer, her hand gripping the shelf she had fallen back against as he continued, "That's why in the end we went with a small gold heart for the mass production." He motioned for her to turn around so he could latch the necklace on her. She spun around, allowing him to, and she felt his lips touch her neck once he finished.

"Now you and I have something that is just for us," he whispered, turning her back around to face him, and he pulled out the gold she had caught when he leaned forward. It was her necklace.

"You—" She couldn't finish the sentence and reached out to touch the necklace on his chest.

"I thought you said I would always be your ult bias and you would continue to support me." He crossed his arms and his jaw clenched in frustration again. "Have you not noticed I haven't stopped wearing it?"

"I—" she didn't want to lie. She had noticed, but she thought it was simply coincidence and that the stylist had picked a similar piece. She nodded.

His hand grabbed the sides of her chin to pull her face up toward his.

"Use your words, 애기." His lips teased her.

"I noticed," she blurted instantly. "I noticed and hoped for it to be mine, but I thought it might've just been your stylist making the choice."

His lips crashed hard on hers again. His tongue not asking for entrance but pushing in as he pressed her against the shelf where she heard several items rattling from his force. He pulled away to allow them both air, his forehead leaning on hers.

"Now let's pick some flowers to make this the most memorable necklace photograph you ever take," his husky hungry voice all but moaned.

She laughed as she walked back over to the boxes with him in tow to sort through all the boxes. She never expected that one night would change her life forever. But as she looked to her side to see the brightest smile on the lips of her ultimate bias, 지훈, she realized one night had in fact changed the whole trajectory. She had convinced herself to walk away from him because she believed he was so unobtainable, so out of reach that there was no way he would want more than a night with her. She bottled up the fact that she had fallen in love with him that night.

Yet there he was, after professing he was also in love with her, helping her pick fake flowers for a necklace he made specifically for their memory.

"사랑해," he whispered, pulling out several hues of pink peonies and turning to look at her. Her eyes went wide, not only at being caught staring but at his simple but strong profession of love.

"사랑해," she responded, leaning over and pecking him on the lips. "Let's get this finished as fast as possible so I can show you just how much."

The End

KOREAN VOCABULARY:

마자 – maja – correct
　보고 싶어 – bogo sip-eo – I miss you
　나도 – nado – me too
　사랑해 – saranghae – I love you

WANT CLARıT MERCH?

https://ko-fi.com/koreanfromcontext/shop

ACKNOWLEDGMENTS

Wow. Another acknowledgment page?! I still get shocked when I finish another book. Always, the first person I must thank is my husband. The man who brings me coffee, water, and food when I'm too focused to maintain the sustenance myself. The man who is my constant source of inspiration. I love you mi amor.

My parents, WHO SHOULD NEVER EVER READ THIS BOOK EVER, but who also continue to support me and my dreams.

Morrigan, a new friend, but one I know is going to be around for a long time. Thank you for challenging me and pushing me to do sprints after work and on weekends to get this novella done in the quickest amount of time I've ever written a book.

Thank you to my first ever round of BETA readers. I think you helped me make this the best novella it could possibly be.

Thank you to all the friends. From the ones I've know since elementary school to the one's I have met on this writing journey, who have inspired characters and stories, who have picked me up when I was down, who help me even when they don't even know it.

To everyone who purchases this book and the next FIVE in the series, thank you as well.

TO EVERYONE, 고마워요!

FOLLOW ME

Website: koreanfromcontext.com
Instagram: @koreanfromcontext
Tiktok: @koreanfromcontext
Twitter: @koreanfrmcntxt
Buy Me A Kofi: https://ko-fi.com/koreanfromcontext

OTHER WORKS

Seoul Searching
Matching Set
An Afternoon In Monaco (available on Kofi)
Traveler (available on Kindle Vella)

Printed in Great Britain
by Amazon

43205073R00067